PADS, PURSES, AND PLUM PUDDING

A PADDY'S PEELERS MYSTERY
BOOK TWO

AUBREY WYNNE

Editing by The Editing Hall
Paddy's Peelers Logo Art by Jaycee DeLorenzo

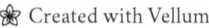 Created with Vellum

SERIES LIST

Keep updated on future releases, exclusive excerpts, and prizes by following my newsletter:
https://www.subscribepage.com/k3f1z5

Once Upon a Widow series (sweet Regency)
Earl of Sunderland #1
A Wicked Earl's Widow #2
Rhapsody and Rebellion #3
Earl of Darby #4
Earl of Brecken #5
Earl of Griffith #6
Beware a Wallflower's Wrath #7
A Wallflower's Wassail Punch #8
The Scoundrel's Christmas Challenge #9
The Duplicate Duke #10
Kiss the Scoundrel Farewell #11

A Paddy's Peelers Mystery series
Crime, Conspiracies, and Courtship #1
Pads, Purses, and Plum Pudding #2

Poisons, Potions, and Parasols #3

Read on Kindle Unlimited

A MacNaughton Castle Romance (steamy Regency Highland series)

A Merry MacNaughton Mishap (Prequel) (only sweet romance in series)

Deception and Desire #1

Allusive Love #2

A Bonny Pretender #3

SUMMARY

Dr. Sampson Brooks is on a case that has nothing to do with medicine. He vows to help bring down the man who ruined his father and sent his mother to an early grave. When the villain's top henchmen are apprehended, Sam attends the hanging. While closing one chapter of his story, he unexpectedly opens another.

Dottie Brown, young and naïve, is duped by a charming swindler. A year after the wedding, she learns he's not what he pretends to be. Watching him on the gallows, she vows never to be taken in by romantic notions again. Yet fate tosses two obstacles in her path that day—a handsome physician and an abandoned child.

A chance encounter reveals one woman's secret, another man's revenge, and a love that will change their lives forever.

FOREWORD

The Oxford English Dictionary defines *underworld* as: 1. Sublunary or terrestrial world. 4.a. A sphere or region lying or considered to lie below the ordinary one. Hence also (figurative) a lower, or the lowest, stratum of society 4.b. The world of criminal or of organized crime (usually with the); hence, the inhabitants of this region.

This was the world of Paddy's Peelers.

* * *

"For alongside the world of Pride and Prejudice and the Nature poets there existed a pulsating, undisciplined urban underworld of young thieves, body-snatchers and gamblers. Pleasure-seekers and criminals alike were enjoying a final fling before the coming of the Metropolitan Police in 1829. Gambling and drinking were endemic in upper- and lower-class society, fraud in the middle classes."

Donald A Low *The Regency Underworld*

THE STORY OF PADDY'S PEELERS

peeler, n. 1816

...Originally: a member of the Irish constabulary. Later: (more gen.) a police officer; spec. a member of the original London Metropolitan force...

Patrick O'Brien, previously of the Dublin Police Force, left Dublin with his wife Margaret and arrived in London in 1798. Paddy was frustrated with the lack of government involvement in crime and the poor, unreliable pay received by officers. He wanted to belong to an organized body of policing.

Margaret's stepbrother worked as a Bow Street Runner, and this new policing force greatly interested O'Brien. It was directly attached to the magistrates and court, housed at 4 Bow Street, and received some funds from the central government through grants. The Runners were to become the model of the future, proving to the government and the public that a professional police force could reduce crime.

O'Brien soon gained a reputation at the Bow Street court for his clever and expedient investigations. While his professional life provided him great satisfaction, his personal life was lacking. He and his wife lamented the absence of children in their household.

When Paddy stumbled across a sick waif in an alley in Whitehall, he brought the lad home. Over the years, their "family" grew to a brood of seven. The couple developed the unique talents of their six boys and one girl, eventually creating a detective agency as the children grew into adulthood. The men would spend an allotted time as a constable for Bow Street while working in the "family business."

Nicknamed Paddy's Peelers (*peeler* slang for an Irish policeman), O'Brien's crew became an efficient team that included detectives, a physician who doubled as a coroner for autopsies, a solicitor who specialized in criminal law, a female master of disguise able to infiltrate any level of society, and a barrister who later joined their ranks to present certain cases pro bono in a High Court.

PROLOGUE

Christmas Eve 1802
East London

A mist of icy rain coated Sam's thin jacket and seeped into his cracked shoes. He was so cold. His stomach hurt. He had nowhere to go. Approaching footsteps—at least two sets—echoed eerily behind him, so he turned a corner and hurried into a dark alley. With his back to the slimy wall, he watched three dark forms pass him.

Sam had no money for them to steal, but they'd take his coat and shoes. He slid to the ground, leaning against a cluster of barrels, and closed his eyes. Just for a moment. Just until he could figure out where to go. His trembling hands pulled the coat tightly around his neck, and he huddled with his head against his knees, feeling his warm breath go through the ragged wool of his breeches.

. . .

"*Sam, would you light the plum pudding?*" *His mother's soft voice matched the gentle touch on his shoulder. She was so beautiful in the deep-blue silk gown that matched her shining eyes.*

He looked to his father, excitement rising in his chest. "Sir?"

"You're a young man of ten—almost eleven now, Sampson." There was an odd catch to his father's voice that Sam had rarely heard. Smoothing his thick black hair, his father tugged on his brocade waistcoat before continuing, "It's time you took on more responsibility and learned your place in the world. Don't you agree, Mrs. Brooks?"

His mother blinked rapidly and nodded. "Yes, dear."

To Sam's surprise, she pulled him into a tight hug. Pressing her lips to his forehead, she whispered, "Remember, we love you very much."

"Mama, don't overset yourself." He gave her a peck on the cheek as she poured brandy into a cup. He gave his father a side-glance with his eyebrow raised, wondering why they were both so out of character tonight. "It must be the holiday making you both sentimental."

A thought struck him. "It isn't because I'll be going off to Winton next fall? I'll always be home for Christmastide."

"Of course you shall!" His father slapped Sam on the back and handed his wife the sprig of holly to place on top of the dessert. "But this will be the last Christmas... well... as we have known them. You're becoming a man, and someday, God willing, you'll have your own house with your own family. Life can change in the blink of an eye or the stroke of a pen..." Mr. Brooks blinked and turned toward the window.

Mrs. Brooks smiled brightly. "No dour thoughts tonight, my love. Let us enjoy the festivities."

His father retrieved the tinder box from the mantel and handed it to his son. Sampson poured the brandy over the dessert, a smile turning up his mouth as the liquor pooled around the bottom of the plate. It was a fine brandy—his father had taught him the difference between the smooth and cheap blends.

"Papa?" Given a nod of approval, Sam pulled a slender pine stick from the box and held it to the hearth fire. The brimstone at the end flared yellow and orange. He slowly turned and touched the burning end to the pool of brandy surrounding the dessert.

With a loud poof! the plum pudding was surrounded in flames. He held his breath as the dessert flickered, the pungent scent of brandy mixing with the sweetmeats. The Brooks family laughed and clapped, Mr. and Mrs. Brooks kissed, then hugged their son, and wished one another a happy Christmas. As his mother cut each of them a slice, his father poured the wine.

It was the best day of the year for Sam. He had received his own writing set, with a bottle of ink and a journal to write in. "For your memories, ponderances, and the most valuable lessons you shall learn in life," his father had said when he'd opened the gift.

After they finished eating, they gathered around the harpsichord. His mother's slender fingers touched the wooden keys lovingly, then impatiently brushed at a tear rolling down her pink cheek. With a deep breath, her fingers hit the keys with gusto, playing "While Shepherds Watched Their Flocks" as they all sang. Afterwards, his parents took their chairs before the fire, waiting for Sampson to read to them.

He settled on the plush rug, leaning against his mother's legs, and opened the Bible to a marked section in the Book of Matthew. The story of Nazareth and the babe born in a stable was always the crown on the evening. The fire crackled cheerily before them, faces of family now gone watching over them from the mantel.

Sampson cleared his throat as he always did before reading aloud, then paused. He looked up at his father, pride beating in his chest for the man who had begun life as a coal boy and now was a prosperous merchant. His mother was known as the Beautiful Mrs. Brooks. Sampson would continue to improve the family name by *attending Winton, moving on to university, then studying at the Inns of Court. There, he would study law and become a solicitor. Make his father proud. Oh, how he wanted to be as respected and successful as his father.*

"Papa, tell me again what my days will be like at Winton?" He would begin the Michaelmas term in October. It seemed more like years rather than months away.

"Well, first of all, you'll become accustomed to a new routine. Your studies will be difficult, but you have a quick mind. I am confident you will—"

A SWIFT KICK to the backside woke Sampson from his dream.

"Well, well, what do we have here?" sneered a voice from the shadows of the alley. "Anything worth my time?"

Sam swiped at his face and squinted at the dark figures hovering over him. The chill, damp stone had soaked through his bones. He tried to sit up, one palm landing in something slick, *what* he didn't want to think about. He wiped his hand against the wooden barrel he'd been leaning on before he fell asleep.

The man wore a filthy wool coat with the collar turned up against the cold. His hair hung from under his cap, greasy strands loose and stuck to the side of his face. Puffs of white floated from his nose when he snorted, still peering down at Sam.

"Leave the lad alone, will ye?" pleaded a woman. She was dressed in a tight gown that exposed her generous bosom. A thin shawl covered her shoulders. "I'm givin' ye what yer lookin' fer. It's Christmas Eve—let the boy be." She whispered something in the man's ear, and he grinned, displaying brownish-gray teeth.

"C'mon then, my little bat. Let's see if yer worth the price."

They moved on, stopping in the blackness at the end of the alley. Their laughter and moans faded as Sam scurried back onto the street. He made his way down Bush Lane, searching for an empty alley where he could hide behind some barrels and wait for the sun to rise. Surely, there would be a few passersby he could beg for some coin from on Christmas Day. His belly growled in agreement.

Only a year ago, he'd been surrounded by loving parents, a fine home, a warm bed, and a promising future. Tonight, he'd be grateful for a chunk of bread and a coat not threadbare, sleeves that covered his arms, and shoes that fit without holes. His stomach growled painfully after the cruel recurring nightmare. The memory of that last dinner of roasted fowl and plum pudding made his mouth water. He chewed on his chapped bottom lip, and it started to bleed. He gagged at the salty, metallic taste.

It had been a nightmare when the constable came to arrest his father. February second, Candlemas Day. In hindsight, he understood the disappearing furniture "out for repair," his mother insisting she enjoyed performing household duties for her "men" as the cook, then the maid quit. The poorer quality of their meals had been explained away by the change in butcher or baker. Yet, Mr. Brooks had refused to sell the harpsichord—his wife's only possession she'd brought into their marriage.

After several months, what little blunt his father had been able to take with him to debtors' prison had been sorely depleted. They'd had to move to more crowded quarters. His mother's cough worsened inside the damp stone walls, shoved together with so many people that there was no room for cots. So, Sam had left the prison and looked for work. At King's Bench, he was one more mouth for his father to feed.

This afternoon, Sam's last coin had gone to his parents, still residing in debtors' prison. It had taken half the day to make it to the Southwark prison and cost a farthing of his precious stolen hoard to see them. But his fragile mother would die in the debtors' prison without a dry place to sleep and sustenance. He'd been horrified to learn that one must pay for everything in gaol. It made no sense. His father was in debt, yet he might never leave the prison walls because all their blunt went to the wardens. Without the payments, his parents would suffer worse conditions in an overcrowded cell, layers of filthy straw for a mattress, fending off even hungrier, more desperate inmates.

He learned to survive. Therefore, his parents would survive. But it was a daily struggle to find a position when one had no manual labor skills, only book learning. Grown men with families claimed any position Sam might have been qualified for.

He tried street sweeping, but he didn't have the gumption for it. The successful boys jumped in front of people, swept a path for them, then demanded or finagled money from the unlucky passersby. He was too big for a chimney sweep. A barkeep gave him a corner in the kitchen in exchange for running errands and tending the fire. With a place to sleep, Sam had held horses for the genteel and sold newspapers on the street during the day. A modiste gave him soup and bread whenever she needed a chore done around her shop. But it was barely enough to keep himself fed and warm, let alone support his parents.

And then the final blow. Last week, a new barkeep had taken over the tavern. He had his own sons to help him, and Sam found himself out on his ear without shelter.

So, much to his horror, he found himself snatching food from stands and running like the thief he'd vowed never to become. At low tide, he joined the other mud larks, combing the Thames's muddy bottom for anything he could sell. His clothes reeked of the foul river, the cuffs of his shirt and hems of his breeches in tatters. His hands and feet blistered from the constant exposure to the frigid water and muck. There, a boy of five had befriended him, offering "trade secrets" on pickpocketing for a share of Sampson's stolen food.

Sampson J. Brooks, once a future solicitor with the world before him, was now a thief and a pickpocket—still an apprentice-in-training for the latter. He hadn't actually picked any pockets or stolen any purses yet. But it had to be better than mud larking. Except his hands shook every time he thought about it.

He saw a lively group in front of a tavern, just off Bush Lane. Maybe someone would drop a coin. He approached the stone building, blending with the rest of the businesses except for the sign above. *The Dog's Bone.*

"Where're ye goin' so early, my friend?" A drunken portly woman called out from a tavern door.

A large man stumbled out, his hand up in a friendly good-night wave, the echo of music and laughter following his huge dark form. "Home. I've a wife waiting. I won't risk her wrath by not being home on Christmas Day."

The murky yellow light spilling from the grimy window framed the customer's silhouette into a giant menacing shadow. Sampson couldn't see his face, but he could feel the strength of the man. But the glint of gold that flashed as the man twirled his walking cane had caught Sam's attention. How much could a cane like that be worth? Enough to feed his parents for a month, he'd wager.

Sam leaned back, blending into the shadows of the stone steps and hoping the man would head his way. He did, weaving ever so slightly across the street toward Sam. Collecting his courage, Sam hid in the dark corner of the stoop, willing the feeling back into his calloused hands. As the gentleman passed by—for he must have been a gentleman from his fine coat, hat, and gleaming boots—Sam prayed to any god listening that the man was foxed.

Slipping from the darkness, Sampson quickly moved behind the tall form, mimicking his victim's walk as the river lad had taught him. When the man leaned to the right, then to the left, so did Sampson. He eyed the walking cane with the gleaming handle and intricately carved stick, knowing it would bring a month's keep at the pawn shop.

He sucked in a deep breath, lunged forward, his hand grasping the stick, and—

"Mother Mary and Joseph. What d'ye t'ink ye're doin', boyo?"

A great paw pulled Sampson up by the back of his collar. It began to rip, and he struggled, praying the cheap wool that had never kept him warm would at least aid in his escape. His feet hit the ground again, and Sam took off once more, only to have the hook of the cane pull him back by his neck.

"Oh-ho. Ye t'ink to get away so easy?" boomed the deep voice.

Sampson raised his head and looked at the barrel-chested Irishman. His brogue was as thick as his red hair and beefy hands. *I'm doomed.* He squeezed his eyes shut, waiting for the sturdy fist to find its target.

He stared at Sam for a while, then gave him another shake.

"Open those eyes, boyo," the stranger demanded. "Ye want to die in a rat-infested prison or be transported to Australia?"

Sam shook his head, terrified of this monstrosity of a man.

"Tis no answer, boyo."

Sam shook his head again, blinking back the hot tears stinging his eyes.

"No tongue? A mute, are ye?"

"No, my lord."

That seemed to amuse the man, for he let out a hearty guffaw. "I'm a hardworkin' Irishman. Not a drop of blue blood in me."

"Yes sir," Sam croaked.

"Da workhouse would give ye a meal and a cot to sleep on."

"I need coin, sir."

He barked a laugh. "Don't we all. Better ways to get it besides robbing a man."

"I've tried, sir," Sam managed, imagining his mother's tearstained face when he never showed up at King's Bench again.

The man's blue eyes narrowed, studying Sam for a long while. Sam held his gaze, waiting to be dragged to the nearest constable. *Why had he tried for that walking stick?*

"So ye have manners, I see. Where'd ye learn 'em?"

"My parents, sir."

"And where might they be?"

"At King's Bench, sir."

Another long stare as Sam fought the urge to squirm.

"How long ye been on da streets?"

"April last, sir."

"What'd ye do before da family was put away?"

"My father owned a bookshop, and I was to start Winton last month." Something in the stranger's tone had changed, sparking a tiny flicker of hope in Sam's chest.

"How long ye been stealin' from honest folks?"

"Except for food from the costermongers—and only the finer dressed ones—you are my first. And I wish to God I could undo it!" he blurted out to his captor. "I swear I'll never do it again."

"Da fat is in da fire, lad." The stranger eased up a bit on the cane around Sam's neck, then snorted. "Do ye want a hot meal and a cot to sleep on?"

Sam nodded his head vigorously, his chin bumping the gold crook of the stick.

"Are ye willin' to work for it?"

Another energetic nod.

"D'ye have a dram of loyalty in yer blood?" asked the burly man.

"At least a barrel, sir, if you don't hand me over to the constable."

"I'll want every drop. I can put ye to work but no tongue waggin'." He squinted at Sam. "I see sumtin' in yer sad eyes, boyo. If I be a bettin' man, I'd say ye learnt some life lessons and will come out da better for it."

Sam hung his head, blinking back pesky tears.

"T'ink about it, boyo—"

"It's Sampson J. Brooks." He looked the Irishman in the eye. "My name is Sampson J. Brooks. I can read, write, and keep a ledger. I've read a dozen books about plants and healing. My brain is quick, but my hands…" He held up his hands, palm up, implying that pickpocketing wasn't his best skill.

"Oh, ho! Well, Sampson, I don't need a thief in my employ." He removed the cane from the boy's neck. "Tis yer lucky day, for I'm goin' to release ye. If ye run, I'll not chase ye. Dat action will tell me ye ain't worth da effort." He nodded and grinned. "If ye come with me, ye get a cot, a warm meal, and Christmas with da most generous and kind woman God's ever seen fit to put on dis earth."

A tear slid down Sam's cheek, and he brushed at it with an angry jerk. He tried to take a deep breath, but a pain shot up his ribs. Could he trust this man? He didn't appear to be an angel. But then, Sam had never seen one except in religious books. He felt the giant paw on his thin shoulder and looked up. It couldn't be worse than gaol.

You have manners, he'd said. Sam did have manners, and he'd make his mother proud.

"I would be honored to accompany you home, sir."

"There's the spirit, boyo. I'm Paddy O'Brien. *Mister* O'Brien to da likes of ye." He chuckled, a warm rumbling sound that made Sam smile too—his first in months. "I think my Maggie will take to ye once she's cleaned ye up."

CHAPTER 1

June 1820
Cheapside, London

The front door opened, bringing with it the clatter of horse hoofs, the stench of the city, and a handsome dark-haired man with a roguish smile. "Luvvy, I'm home."

Mrs. Robert Dunn met him with a grin and wrapped her arms around his neck. "Did you miss me?"

"Always." He gave her a sound kiss, pulling her close and swinging her in a circle before setting her down with a smack on her arse. "I'm afraid I've got some bad news."

Dorothea shook her head. "Not tonight. We are celebrating your return after three long months, and I won't tolerate anything dour." She pulled him to the wingback chair in front of the coal stove. "I'll pour you some brandy."

Robert eased his stocky frame into the chair with a heavy

sigh. "I suppose it can wait. You know how I hated to leave you, but when the man gives orders…" His nostrils twitched and he nodded toward the "kitchen" at the other end of the room. "What magic are you working in there, luvvy?"

A rabbit sizzled over the small hearth fire, and a loaf of bread waited on the table with freshly churned butter. Short-bread—her husband's favorite—was hidden away in a basket. A perfect dinner for their first anniversary. It had been so lonely when Robert had left for Scotland, hauling wagons of goods for his employer, a vicar in Stepney. A child would have eased the emptiness. She brushed back the emotion that threatened whenever she remembered the miscarriage.

But the midwife had said it was not unusual to lose the first, and there was no reason she couldn't have another. And Robert had kept his promise, returning in time for their anniversary. So, she focused on the happiness the future would bring them both. Dorothea untied her apron and eased it over her head, careful not to muss her hair. Arranged in a loose chignon, she took a quick peek at the dulled mirror and pulled down some of her auburn curls to nestle against her cheeks.

"You're wearing my favorite gown," Robert said with a wink. "I thought of your eyes when I bought it." He had given her the deep-blue muslin dress last Christmas. A white satin ribbon emphasized the high waist, and delicate lace bordered the modest neckline and cap sleeves.

"You say that every time I wear it." She had begun sewing tiny delicate birds of peace along the hem. It would be perfect to wear again next Christmastide. The white wings seemed to take flight as she moved across the small parlor to rejoin her husband.

She handed him a cup, and he took it, pulling her onto his lap along with the drink. "I swear you get prettier every day. How did I get so lucky?"

With a laugh, she pushed off his lap. "You charmed me before I knew any better."

"You stole my heart at first glance. I couldn't believe a young beauty would give an old man a second look." He nuzzled her neck, making her giggle. "Remember?"

"How could I forget?"

She had taken some of her students from the Darlington School for Girls into the nearby village. Dorothea, then Miss Brown, had been employed there as an instructor of French, household accounts (knowledge mandatory for every good wife), and the pianoforte. With their proximity to London, many wealthy merchants sent their daughters there for "polish."

"Here I was, minding my own business—"

"Whistling at ladies is not minding your own business," she interrupted with a giggle, stroking her hand through his hair and noticing the added gray in the thinning black.

"Who's telling this story?" Robert's dark eyes twinkled as he tugged on one of her curls. "Here comes this gaggle of girls"—he held up a finger when she opened her mouth—"tittering and pretending not to look at me. Their chaperone is gaping so hard that she trips and falls right into my arms."

She kissed his cheek. "And they lived happily ever after. Even though you were *almost* old enough to be my father."

"It did take six months of wooing to get you to say yes, luvvy."

"Do you regret it?" Why did she always ask him this? Because she'd never expected to find a husband and have a family. A spinster helping other young ladies find happiness had been her future. And she'd been more than satisfied with her lot until Mr. Robert Dunn had burst into her life.

"Never. And you? Are you happy?"

His sudden serious demeanor sent a shiver up her spine.

Something was wrong. *Tomorrow. Ask tomorrow.* "Only one thing could make it better," she whispered in his ear.

"That will come, luvvy. In fact, the more we try—"

"The sooner I'll be with child." She grinned as he threw back the whiskey and stood, cradling her in his arms.

"Enough said."

* * *

A WEEK LATER

DR. SAMPSON BROOKS walked across Bush Lane and stopped in front of the Dog's Bone. This tavern had been a beacon of light on a cold Christmas Eve almost eighteen years ago. Tonight, he was meeting Paddy and Walters here for news. The news he'd been waiting for… almost his entire life, or so it seemed. He removed his hat and entered the old building.

He nodded to the brawny bald man behind the counter on his left. "Evening, Leo."

The man grinned at him and pointed to the back. Leo had given up his "office" to the Peelers whenever they needed it. It gave O'Brien's investigators a place to discuss business away from home. It was private, close to home, and Leo served good ale, not the cheap watered down brown liquid found in other riverfront taverns.

The barmaid stopped in front of him, holding several bowls of a rich stew. He was making his way to the back, stopping to say hello to a friend or client. "Ale or porter?" asked Bess.

"Ale, please."

"I'll bring it back as soon as I'm done serving this stew. Did you want any of this?" She raised one of the crocks she was carrying.

"It smells good. Yes, thank you." Sam wouldn't have to stop on the way home for something to eat.

"The Thomases are over there," she informed him with a nod of her head, sending her brown curls bouncing beneath her mobcap. "Want to tell you thank you again."

Sampson stopped at the booth, asking about the couple's youngest, who he'd seen for a fever last week. They were a good family, and he'd allowed Mrs. Thomas to fix meals for him last week to pay for his services. He grinned. While some thought he was daft for bartering, he enjoyed having his home cleaned, his clothes washed, and meals cooked in exchange for helping the sick. He remembered what it was like to be hungry. And he remembered how much any kindness had been appreciated.

It was funny, when he thought about it, that he'd become a doctor instead of a solicitor. Maggie, his second mother, had known his future before he had. The woman had an uncanny intuition about people. And to her delight, she was rarely wrong.

After several conversations, Sam entered the back room. It was a room that seemed untouched by time. The charred beams overhead and large open hearth on one end spoke of the history of this old inn turned tavern. There were shelves along one stone wall, holding a variety of supplies. A small room off this held Leo's more expensive bottles of liquor and port.

"'Tis about time, boyo," boomed Paddy from a table in the center of the room. "Beginning to t'ink ye were ill yerself." He reached down and scratched the wolfhound often at his side.

"I see you brought Aonarach with you," Sam observed as the giant wire-haired dog stood to greet him. His long gray tail wagged while he enjoyed a good ear scratch.

"Maggie was wanting all da males out o' da house, so I

took my faithful hound and fled." The Irishman held up a bumper of ale and waved it toward Walters. "Did ye order the stew? 'Tis a good one."

Sam nodded and sat across from Harry Walters, his brother by luck as the Peelers always called each other. Harry had been the first waif Paddy had taken off the street. Sam noted a shine in the man's dark eyes.

"Good news, I assume?" Sam asked, leaning over the table and squinting at Walters. "Is that more gray along your temples, Brother? Lady Matilda won't want an old man waiting for her at the altar. Maybe you need to take some time off."

Harry snorted. "It shows more because my hair is so dark. Speaking of age, I see more lines around those *fine hazel eyes* as Bess calls them. Too much winking at the ladies? The gossipmongers have had your name bouncing up and down Cheapside."

"Enough sibling rivalry," interrupted Paddy with a chuckle. "Don't try to stoke my fire, boyos. I'm already old, I have a lovin' woman at home—"

"Who booted us out for the afternoon," reminded Harry.

"True enough," Paddy conceded. A soft knock on the door, then Bess entered with a bumper of ale, a bowl of stew, and a pitcher to refill drinks for the two other men.

"Ye're a vision, my girl," said Paddy. "Any time ye want me to knock some sense into dat big oaf o' mine, just say the word." It was common knowledge that Bess was sweet on Gus, another of the O'Brien clan.

She shook her head, laughter in her brown eyes. "I'll catch him on me own time, thank ye very much. I'm in no hurry, Mr. O'Brien."

Once she left, Sampson took a pull of his ale and waited.

"We've located two of the men involved in the insurance scandal that ruined your father. Robert Dunn was the leader who rented the office and sold your father the fake insurance. The other man printed the certificates and collected the money." Walters paused while Sam took in this information. "They are in London, working with a villain we only know as The Vicar."

"How will we press charges against them for something that happened so long ago?"

"Tis not like da leopards change their spots. Last winter, Dunn was kidnapping chimney sweeps grown too big for da work, stealing boys from one brothel and selling dem to another. Da Home Office wants him for being involved with those Spencean radicals who tried to overthrow da government last winter." Paddy grinned. "Dunn has a long list of unsavory business practices, but treason could be da one to bring him down."

"By stringing him up," Walters added with a snort.

"He was lying low for a while, but he's popped out from his hidey-hole," said Paddy. "I've let the magistrate know we're following them, but their time here in London is coming to an end."

"They've been working with two others—a petty thief and his son. I acted as a house thief, looking to pass on stolen goods. They paid me in bad coin," continued Walters. "I plan on meeting up with them again at the Rat's Nest. If I get another counterfeit coin, I'll set someone on them. If we can find out where they're minting them, it will be easier to make the arrest."

"If Dunn catches wind of you, he'll run again," said Sam. "If there's anything I can do to help…"

"A taste of the waste makes a thief of the beast as Maggie always says," quoted Walters. "He's been out of action too long. The mangy cur's used to making good blunt and itching to fill his pockets again. And a pretty little wife to support."

"I'll make sure ye're at Bow Street when we bring dem in, Sam," Paddy assured him. "But breathe easy now, knowing yer retribution is close at hand."

* * *

July

DOROTHEA SAT IN THE ROCKER, mending some socks, humming an old tune her mother used to sing to her as a child. A knock on the door interrupted her musings. When she answered, Mr. Cotter, one of the local constables, stood before her, hat in hand.

"Beg your pardon, Mrs. Dunn. May I come in?" His stern look made her stomach clench.

"What's wrong? Is it Robert? Is he hurt?" Panic skittered up her spine as the older man walked past her. His short gray hair was tousled by the strong winds of the day, and he stood rigid by the door.

"No, ma'am. I need... to speak with him." She shut the door as two men passed by, giving her a side-glance. The taller man, older with red hair, caught her gaze and held it for a brief moment. She slammed the door against the overwhelming sense of danger.

"I'm afraid Mr. Dunn isn't home yet. I expect him soon, though. Would you like to wait?"

Mr. Cotter bobbed his head. "Yes, ma'am. Thank you."

"I'll fix us some tea while we—"

"No need, Mrs. Dunn." He averted her gaze when she gave him a questioning look.

The heavy silence set off more warning bells. Did this have something to do with the "bad news" Robert had wanted to tell her on their anniversary? She had never brought the subject up again. Was he in some kind of trouble? She knew little of his position with the man she knew only as the vicar. It paid well, but he kept irregular hours. Robert said his employer was very private, and he often had to go out in the middle of the night to assist distraught parishioners.

The door burst open, and Robert rushed through it, an unfamiliar air of urgency sweeping in with him. "We have to pack, luvvy. I don't have time to explain, but we need—"

He froze, taking in the constable standing near the stove. "Ah, Mr. Cotter," he said, his tone smoothing out, the familiar Robert returning. "How's the missus? That boy of yours sure is growing."

"None o' that will be necessary. I'm afraid you know why I'm here." The constable moved forward. "Let's make this easier on your wife and come along quietly."

"No! There must be some mistake." She looked wildly from her husband to Mr. Cotter, their friend. "He's done nothing wrong."

When she locked her gaze on Robert, her stomach roiled. His dark eyes were black and cold as a moonless winter night. She didn't know this man who stood before her. Her Robert was warm and kind and charming. This man…

"Robert?" she asked in a quivering voice, her hand finding the back of a chair to hold her up. "What have you done?"

"Don't look at me like that." He sneered. "You've enjoyed all the finery I've given you, the life you've had with me. Do you think it comes without a price?"

"But you work for a man of God…" Dorothea shook her head. None of this made any sense.

"The Vicar is no man of God, ma'am," said Mr. Cotter. "He's the head of a criminal ring, and your husband is one of his best henchmen."

Robert made a dash for the door, Dorothea screamed, and

the constable cursed. A scuffle in the alley, more cursing, followed by "Where ye off to in such a hurry, boyo?"

She ran outside to see the redheaded man and his partner dragging her husband away. Her breaths came in rapid spurts as she cried out, then all went black.

CHAPTER 2

End of July 1820
Newgate Prison

"What will happen to you now?" Dorothea asked, though she already knew the answer.

The nightmares came every night—the rope swinging, Robert's feet dangling. The fear that after all this time, she might be pregnant—and alone.

She still couldn't reconcile this man before her with the charismatic gentleman she'd married. The dazzling smile that had melted her heart, soft kisses that promised a happy future. What a fool she'd been. What a monster he was.

"We both know my fate, luvvy," he said softly.

"Don't call me that. Don't ever call me that again." But she had to ask, had to know for sure. "Is it true? You've kidnapped children and killed men? For some mysterious employer who goes by the ridiculous moniker of The Vicar?"

"Careful, now. He's a dangerous man with a network of

criminals to do his bidding and spies all over London. Keep your mouth shut or they'll find you floating in the Thames." Robert scowled, then answered her with a heavy sigh. "I killed my first man when I was ten. It was him or me. The Vicar kept me from hanging, so I was told, and I've been working for him ever since. Worked my way up."

"To kidnapping little boys and girls?"

"That was a side job to tide me over, waiting for the real blunt. We took the boys from one flash house and sold them to another. They were already in hell. We just swapped them to another for a price. I do as I'm told." His eyes pleaded with her to forgive or at least understand, the softness returning to his gaze. "It means a lot that you came to see me one last time."

"I came for answers, to try to make sense of this before…" She turned her head, blinking back the tears.

"Did you get the money?" he asked, as if that would make it all better.

She nodded, feeling the heat in her cheeks. One of Robert's "associates" had brought her his last wages with a promise of a "widow's pension." Dorothea had wanted to throw the pouch of coins back in the man's face, but common sense won out. She had to eat. "I have to be out by the end of the week."

"Will you go back to the school? You seemed happy there," he said, trying to smile.

"Ha! She can't take me back now. I'll soon be the widow of a murderer and a thief." She closed her eyes, praying for the strength to get through this visit, this week, this year. "In fact, no one seems to want to hire me or be associated with 'trouble.' I'm-I'm scared a-and I'll *never* forgive you."

That hard glint was back, his eyes as shiny as a watching crow. Dorothea shivered. She'd been happy at the Darlington

School for Girls. Content and useful. He'd burned that bridge for her.

"Did you ever love me?" Why did it matter? She wouldn't believe a syllable he uttered.

"I believe you are the only person on this earth I've ever loved. When I was with you, I *was* the man I pretended—dreamed—of being." He stood, gave her a heartbreaking smile, and walked away.

"And now I dream of the gallows." A tear slipped down her cheek. Not for the loss of this man, this stranger, but for the loss of her innocence and the abrupt end of her fairy tale. The realization that the world wasn't a wonderful place. It was its own kind of purgatory, and she'd have to bide her time and become a fighter. Or she'd never survive.

* * *

AUGUST 1820
Newgate Prison gallows

SAMPSON DIDN'T USUALLY ATTEND public hangings, but this one was an exception. He stared at the fifteen men lined up on the gallows, understanding the fear in their eyes. It was frightening to meet your maker before you could atone for your sins. Those men would never have the opportunity. Only panicked mumbles as they prayed along with the priest.

He had helped put three of them on that platform, a small part of The Vicar's vast network. Sam had taken off the physician's hat he usually wore when assisting the O'Brien Investigative Service. Nicknamed Paddy's Peelers, Sam's brothers and sister worked to rid the streets of London of thieves and murderers. Patrick O'Brien had come from Ireland to join the

Bow Street Runners and had slowly begun his own agency, acquiring a reputation for thorough investigations. Now a retired Runner, Paddy and his "adopted" family had built a name for themselves by assisting local magistrates in tracking down villains. When the magistrate couldn't find a criminal, they called in Paddy and his Peelers to track them down. Many private citizens often went straight to O'Brien and saved time.

"Lookin' for some entertainment after the 'angin'?"

He looked down at the doxie, gave her a half smile, and shook his head. "This is enough excitement for me."

Turning away from her and pushing into the crowd, he tried to tune out the festive chatter, shouts of vendors, and a fiddle playing somewhere behind him. He was concentrating on the men standing on the far right of the gallows. Only two were responsible for selling the fake certificate of insurance to Sam's father, but all three worked for the mysterious Vicar. Dunn had overseen half his operations in Town. It would cause a large hole in the criminal network.

"Good riddance," Sampson mumbled as the trap doors opened, and the crowd roared their approval. He turned abruptly and pushed his way back through the cheering throng. Another battle won, but the war raged on. But today, Dr. Sampson Brooks had found retribution, and he said a small prayer of thanks. "Rest in peace now," he whispered softly to his dead parents.

* * *

Dorothea stood alone in a multitude of people, clutching her shawl at her neck against the strong gust. The crowd watched the gallows in excitement, waiting for the men to swing in the wind. She, on the other hand, just wanted this chapter of her life to end. She had moved to another part of Cheapside, remained a widow, but took back her surname.

She had been fairly isolated when she was married, preferring to play the wife. To her surprise, few people recognized her when she introduced herself as Mrs. Dottie Brown. They would have turned their back on Mrs. Robert Dunn.

She'd changed in the past few weeks, no longer humming as she worked, no longer eager to see what was around the next corner. She had a plan. Earn enough money and move to America. No one would know her, no one would care about her past, and no one would ever break her heart again.

A disturbance ahead caught her attention. A man pushed through the mass of people, shouting and cursing. At the same time, Dottie felt a small hand slip into hers. She looked down to see a girl, perhaps six or seven, gazing up at her with huge doe eyes. Her dress was tattered and dirty, her hair uncombed and greasy. The round face was streaked with dirt and… tears?

As the irate man shoved past them, she hid her face in Dottie's skirts.

"Are you alright?" she asked the girl.

The waif shook her head, then peeked over her shoulder to watch the man disappear in the sea of spectators. She studied Dottie a moment before pointing to the men on the scaffold.

Dottie's heart cracked a little more. "Your father is up there?"

The girl shook her head.

"Your brother?"

She nodded and gripped Dottie's hand more tightly, her eyes pinned on the young man next to Robert on the platform.

A loud *slam* and the men dropped. Dottie closed her eyes against the sight and pulled the girl into her skirts. It was over. Time to start again.

A tall, handsome gentleman with brown hair and hazel

eyes paused in front of them. Their eyes met as he passed, and she had the feeling she knew him. Where they would have met, she had no idea. But Dottie was drawn to him in the oddest way. He studied her for a moment as if he, too, found her familiar. With a murmured, "Ma'am," and a tip of his hat, he melted into the crowd.

Dottie looked down at the girl with a raised brow. The street urchin nodded, and in silent agreement, the two lonely females left the gallows behind them.

* * *

CHEAPSIDE

They walked toward her new home—a cozy room attached to the kitchen of a public house. The owner's wife gave her a place to stay in exchange for baking bread and helping with the cooking. Dottie had a warm bed and a kitchen at her disposal to make her various pastries, which she sold on Gracechurch Street to the busy shoppers. On Sundays, she went to St. James's Park where the promenade was crowded with people.

Dottie enjoyed baking, finding it therapeutic as she kneaded the dough and pounded out her frustrations and emotions. She was already making a small profit. Though she hadn't wanted to take her husband's money made by illegal gains, there would have been no way to buy the equipment and ingredients needed to start her business.

She looked down at the small girl beside her. "We haven't even introduced ourselves. How remiss of me." Dottie forced a smile. "I'm Mrs. Brown. What is your name?"

The child gazed around, spotted a flower vendor, and pointed.

"A guessing game, is it?" She pondered the array of flowers. "Daisy?"

The girl shook her head.

"Violet?" This time, the child managed a weak smile and nodded.

"That's a fine name. Violet. I like the sound of it. It may suit you once you're cleaned up." She studied her new young friend. "Do you speak?"

Violet shook her head, giving Dottie a woeful look, then gripped her forearm with both hands.

Dottie sighed. "I won't send you off. No reason for both of us to be alone. But it all depends on the landlady. We'll have to think of something to tell her, other than we met at a hanging."

Violet nodded, a wide grin transforming her round face. She threw her arms around Dottie, almost toppling them both over. "Goodness, child. Don't send us both to the infirmary with your gratitude."

But Violet had made her heart lighter, and she felt a genuine smile curve her lips for the first time in a month. It felt good. Right. She'd think of something to tell Mrs. Clatterly.

The tavern was busy, and Dottie ushered Violet into her room. "Strip off those filthy clothes, and I'll fetch water for a bath."

Violet shook her head. Disgust curled her lip.

"This is not a choice. If you wish to remain a grubby waif, then off you go. I'll not share my bed unless you're clean, and I've combed your hair for lice."

Violet sighed, her small shoulders drooping.

"Well, that wasn't much of a fight. Good." Dottie went out to the pump for water and to find a tub.

When she returned, the girl was inspecting the room, drawing a finger over the wood chair, walking to the bed, and pushing on the mattress, a surprised smile lighting her face.

"Do you approve?"

Violet nodded, undressed with no modesty, and stepped into the small tub. She gasped as water was unceremoniously dumped on her head.

"Gracious me. Your hair is blonde!"

An hour later, Violet sat on a stool in front of Dottie, wearing an old shift that had been cut at the bottom. The girl would need clothes. Dottie had refused to wear mourning for a man she had never really known and went with the story that she'd been widowed over a year. Instead, she'd sold her more impractical dresses except for one her father had given her. With the money, she'd bought sturdier material of brown, dark blue, and gray for clothes that would last longer through the summer and winter months.

"I have some material tucked away. You'll have a new dress by the end of the week. We can take in this old shift and perhaps make a cap from the half I cut off."

Violet nodded, yawned, and leaned back against Dottie's legs while she brushed out her hair. Within minutes, she snored quietly. What kind of life had the girl had before today? Fate had sent her, and Dottie would heed the call. She was lonely, and if Violet wanted to stay, they'd find a way. Perhaps Violet could help her atone for Robert's past.

That night, after a supper of bread, cold meat, and cheese —which Violet stuffed into her mouth like a squirrel storing nuts—they curled up together in the small bed. She had a good start on a dress, and the girl's tattered clothes had been washed and hung to dry. She'd cut the old sleeves and hem shorter, removing the ragged edges so the gown didn't look quite so bad. There was nothing to do for the stains, but at least the child would smell better.

It was the first night she did not dream of the gallows. Instead, she was running in a field of violets, laughing and swinging a little blonde girl in a circle. They fell onto the soft grass—

"Mrs. Brown!" *Thump, thump, thump.* "Mrs. Brown, I hate to bother you."

Dottie woke with a start. "Coming, Mrs. Clatterly. Just a moment." Had she overslept?

Violet stirred and made a snuffling sound, her eyelids fluttering, then rolled over as Dottie rose from the bed. She opened the door to find a frazzled landlady.

"I'm sorry to bother ye, but Mr. Clatterly's leg is acting up again. When it gets this bad, he's got to stay off it until the swelling goes down." She pushed a gray curl under her mobcap and shook her head. "I'm in a pickle. Is there any way you could take over the kitchen this morning while I stay out with the patrons? I can find some extra help later today, so I won't trouble you tomorrow."

"Of course, ma'am. You've been so kind. I'd be happy to help out."

"Oh, you're an angel, you are. Once you're dressed, I'll show you what I've got started. Then I'll ready the public room for the early customers. I have several who come to take breakfast." She scurried away, then returned. "And please help yourself too. Thank you, again."

Though a bum leg wasn't ideal for Mr. Clatterly, it was the perfect opportunity to install Violet as a scullery maid. Once she had a stool so she could reach the sink, the girl washed dishes with gusto. There was a constant smile on her face, making her brown eyes twinkle.

Mrs. Clatterly took to her instantly. "Where'd you find this pretty little thing?"

Dottie was ready with her story. "My late husband's sister had some... debts. I've written to relations, but if you don't mind her staying with me until we hear from someone? She doesn't mind helping out." Though she hated to lie, she

41

couldn't say she'd found the waif when she said goodbye to her husband at the gallows.

"No trouble at all. In debtors' prison, is she? Poor thing. Horrible places, I've heard."

Dottie said a quick prayer of thanks for finding the Clatterlys and began chopping carrots for the day's soup. By the time she'd finished with the landlady's work, she was running late and hurriedly packed her cart with her berry tarts and pasties.

"I'll be back soon," she told Violet, who nodded with a smile.

She wondered about her new companion and whether she'd ever spoken. Had something happened or was she born that way? Dottie would ask her tonight. Perhaps she was just extremely shy. She'd known a girl at the school who rarely spoke, and when she did, it was in a whisper.

The weather was cooler today, so there were more people strolling the graveled paths of St. James's Park. She had sold half the tarts and most of her shortbread when she spied a familiar gentleman approaching on horseback.

The handsome man from... The thought of Newgate made her stomach clench, and she turned her head to avoid meeting his eyes should he look her way. But as the *clip clop* of horses' hooves grew nearer, she took a deep breath.

CHAPTER 3

Early September 1820
St. James's Park, London

Sam had promised to meet Walters that afternoon. *Sir* Harry Walters, he still had to remind himself, was bringing his fiancée for a promenade. Walters wasn't comfortable mingling with the *ton* at Hyde Park, so he agreed to St. James. He told Sam they could enjoy a break from the heat, keep his promise to escort Lady Matilda Bancroft for a Sunday stroll, and pass on some information for another case. Sam, however, expected to find not only the couple, but a "friend" who'd just happened by. Lady Matilda seemed intent on finding him a wife since he'd mentioned it may be time to think of the future.

He leaned down and patted his gelding's neck. "Well, Jack, let's see what tortures await us along The Mall, shall we?" As he urged the bay horse forward, a costermonger caught his attention. The woman selling cake seemed familiar... The moment he recognized her, his heart began to pound. The beautiful woman from Newgate! She'd taken his breath away the instant he'd passed her, even with her red-rimmed eyes. A girl, perhaps her daughter, had held her hand. What had she been doing there? Had a family member or friend been on the gallows? He doubted it had been for entertainment since she'd obviously been crying.

That same odd feeling engulfed Sam again—as if he should know her. Or did know her. Or *would* know her.

"Well, let's take a closer look." Before he reached her cart, he dismounted and spotted the tarts and shortbread. Tarts were his favorite. It seemed fate meant for them to meet.

"Good day, ma'am," he said, eyeing the sweets. "What kind of"—cornflower blue eyes met his, and his lungs seized for a moment—"eyes do you have?"

"The last time I looked they were blue," she quipped, arching an auburn brow.

"Tarts. I mean, tarts." *Beefwit! Stop acting like a green boy.*

She smiled, lighting her up her already perfect heart-shaped face. "The last of the berry and some fine shortbread. What's your preference?"

You.

"A tart, please. I've been partial to those and plum pudding since I was a wee lad." He took the tart, the sugar baked on top glistening in the afternoon sun, and handed her coin as he took a bite.

"That's too much, my lord," he heard her say. But his eyes were closed as the berries and sweet pastry hit his tongue.

He shook his head. "I'd pay twice that for one of these." Licking his lips, he grinned at her.

"I'd be happy to give you another to take with you for that price. Or would you like some shortbread?" Her head tilted as she asked, and he spied her slender neck. Imagined placing kisses along its graceful arch. *Blast! She's most likely married.*

"I'd wager your husband is one happy man." Her expression almost made him curse out loud. *Nodcock!*

"I'm a widow." Her tone was subdued, and her gaze flickered to him and then to the ground. With a forced smile, she lifted the shortbread. "Why don't you try it?"

"I'm sorry. I didn't mean to—"

"It's fine. You meant no harm, my lord." Her lovely cheeks turned pink.

"I'm no lord. Dr. Sampson Brooks at your service." He extended his hand, putting on the charming smile that always worked for his patients.

"Mrs. Brown," she said, taking his hand.

At the touch of her palm, a jolt of pleasure shot up his arm. A sensation he'd never experienced. It was exciting and terrifying. His mother's words came back to him from long ago.

I KNEW your father was the one the moment he kissed my hand. A woman just knows.

WHAT ABOUT MEN? Did a man *just know*? Sam realized she was waiting for him to release her hand, but he was still gripping her fingers. His cheeks burned until she laughed. A sound so sweet that it put him at ease, and he found himself chuckling along with her.

"I believe I will try that shortbread. You seem to have a magic touch." He rolled his eyes, still feeling the warmth of her skin on his. "With tarts, er, baking."

"Thank you, Dr. Brooks. I'll accept the compliment." She handed him the bread. "Enjoy your ride."

"Yes, ma'am—Mrs. Brown," he returned, tipping his hat. "I hope we meet again."

"I'm here every Sunday. Bring your friends." She wiggled her eyebrows. "The more the merrier as they say."

Sam walked away, leading Jack with one hand and eating the shortbread with the other. Once inside the park, he spotted Walters and waved. The lovely blonde next to him also lifted her arm in greeting, but it was the unfamiliar raven-haired woman who had Sam's jaw clenched. He knew this had been a ruse.

"Brooks! Good to see you," Walters said a little too enthusiastically. His stiff smile told Sam that his brother had been duped as well. "We just happened to meet up with—" He looked questioningly at Lady Matilda.

"Dr. Brooks, may I present Miss Halden? Her father is—"

"A banker. I believe I met Mr. Halden at a meeting of the Magdalen Hospital." He bowed to the pretty lady. "It's a pleasure." He would cut this off as soon as politely possible. He preferred lighter hair and more petite, curvy women to the willowy dark type before him.

"Oh yes, the home for wayward women. How generous of you to help such a charity."

"We must all do our part," Sam agreed, stepping back beside his brother.

"I've a favor to ask," Walters said quietly as they all proceeded to move forward, the ladies in front.

"Of course. A case?" he asked, keeping his voice low so the ladies in front of them would not overhear.

"Yes. He was an informant, one of the men who led me to Dunn. His son was on the gallows." Walters let out a sigh. "Seems the young think they're invincible. Ferguson, his father, tried to get the lad to quit with him, but he wouldn't give up the high wage."

"It seems money can destroy as much as help the poor." Sampson saw too many going hungry, taking deadly risks for a day's pay. "I'm sorry for the man and his son."

"Well, it looks like my informant hasn't fared much better. His landlady came to see Paddy. Said Ferguson hadn't been home in days, and the rent was due. She knew the son's fate, and thought Paddy could find something out."

"I suppose she didn't want to rent out the room if he was still alive," offered Sam.

"He was found floating in the Thames, and they needed someone to identify the body. The landlady obliged and verified the dead man was Ferguson."

"Do you think he knew too much? Was he involved with any of the other cases?" Sam knew how the thieves and gangs of the rookeries often crossed paths with violent results. "Perhaps he ran afoul with someone from another rookery."

Walters shrugged. "Don't know. But the landlady is certain he was murdered, and I tend to agree. He was wearing a new wool coat—in August."

"To stay warm in the Thames?" Sam shook his head. "People with little money don't spend it on winter clothes while it's still summer. They live hand-to-mouth and day-to-day. Where is he?"

"At the London hospital until day after tomorrow. Birnie released the body, and the cadaver will be given to one of those anatomy schools."

Richard Birnie was the Bow Street magistrate. Sam assumed the body was being held as a favor. Unless there were extenuating circumstances, an autopsy would be an added expense. The destitute, unless obviously murdered or afflicted with a plague-like disease, weren't considered important enough for such a procedure.

"*One of those anatomy schools* is the reason we are making

such strides in the field of medicine," Sam said. "I'll be sure to stop by tomorrow, and be sure to thank Mr. Birnie for the extra time."

"Thank you." Walters nodded. "And I didn't mean to ambush ye. Mattie didn't tell me of her scheme until we were stepping from the carriage."

"Your gut doesn't talk to you where your lady is concerned." Sam slapped Harry on the back. "You can usually smell a trap and figure a way around it."

Walters, a stocky barrel-chested master of disguise, was the lead investigator for the Peelers. His work to uncover a plot to murder the Prime Minister and all the British cabinet members, now dubbed the Cato Street Conspiracy, had earned him a knighthood. That had given him the courage to court an earl's sister, though Lord Darby was also a friend as well as a previous client.

Harry grinned, his eyes lingering on the backs of the women in front of them. They stepped up to flank the females.

"Ladies," Sam said with a bow, "I'm afraid I must leave you. It was a pleasure to see you again, my lady, and to meet you, Miss Halden."

"Do not be a stranger," Miss Halden said in a husky voice, her lips in a plump pout. Her dark eyes danced with experience an unmarried woman should not yet have.

Sampson lifted a brow and gave Mattie a side-glance.

Lady Matilda's eyes widened, as if surprised by her friend's flirtatious manner, before turning to Sam. "We shall see you for dinner next week, Dr. Brooks?"

If you don't invite any ladies searching for husbands. "Of course, unless some emergency claims my attention." He walked his horse to the path and mounted, eager to be away. If the woman had been a widow, a dalliance may have been possible. But he wouldn't entertain a young woman intent on marriage. Not yet. He was still building his practice, donating time to hospitals, and keeping ridiculous hours.

He made his way back to Cheapside, passing at St. Mary's Le Bow. It was said anyone born within hearing of its bells was considered a true Cockney. The thought brought to mind Mrs. Brown's cultured speech. How had she ended up as a vendor? The woman was a conundrum.

Sam ambled along the busy thoroughfare in the bustling heart of London's commerce and trade. One could buy anything from hats, cottons, silks, and timepieces to perfumes, stationery, and pianofortes. It was a convenient location for a residence too. The shops stood next to houses and apartments, and many affluent merchants made their homes here. From his bedroom window, he could see the Tower of London on a clear day.

When he reached the fork at Cornhill, he veered left toward Threadneedle Street and the Stock Exchange Coffee House. He often stopped there, for it was near his home on Bishop's Gate, and the food was good at a reasonable price. He tossed his rein to a small boy and gave him a coin.

"A penny now, and another when I return to collect the horse. Understood?" he asked the open-mouthed boy, who stared at the penny but nodded his head. "Good." Another memory from his youth, of holding horses for men dressed to the nines and standing for hours for a ha'penny.

"Afternoon, Doc," the proprietor said in a loud voice over the din of patrons. "Wanted to thank ye. The missus is doing much better."

"Glad to hear it, Max. Could you have Sally bring me a coffee, meat pie, and white soup if you still have it? If not, oyster is fine." He perused the crowded house but didn't find a familiar enough face, so he sat at the end of a long trestle table. He grabbed the Sunday edition of *The Recorder* from the center of the table to occupy him while he waited for his meal.

"Well, if it ain't the 'andsome Dr. Brooks," said a cheerful female from above. He tilted his head and smiled at Sally as she set down his coffee. "I saved ye the last bit 'o white soup. It's beef and kidney pie if that's to yer likin'."

"I would be forever grateful," he answered with a wink.

"Aw, go on with ye," she gushed. "I'll be back in two jiffs."

He returned to the newspaper, letting the din of the coffee house fade into a dull clamor. When the food arrived, he continued to read as he ate. Until a huge paw slapped him on the back.

"Spare a poor man a wee bit o' bread?" Patrick O'Brien loomed over him, his huge frame still as intimidating as it had been when Sam was ten. But now he knew better.

"Ho! Tis a beggar, is he now?" Sam rolled his eyes, hearing his own poor attempt at an Irish brogue.

"Only when needed, boyo," Paddy said as he sat down with a *thump*. "Figured I'd find ye here. Tis Margaret's birthday Sunday next, and she wants all her boys to be with her. Since I can't tell her no, I'm roundin' all of ye up in advance."

The "boys" were the misfits the Irishman had collected over the years. The O'Briens took them in, spending the time to find and develop each boy's strength. As they grew, Paddy turned them into a unique team, creating a detective agency that had a reputation for never failing to solve a case or find their man. Sam had gone to medical school, and besides making a nice living as a physician, he also performed autopsies for the Peelers and London constabularies. In court, he was occasionally an expert witness, testifying with medical opinions and the results of the autopsies he performed. On occasion, he went along with the detectives as an extra man, mostly to treat injuries that may occur.

The agency included several detectives who had all put in time as Bow Street Runners. The O'Briens had also raised a solicitor, whose law expertise helped prepare cases for court, and a woman who'd played so many different parts in Paddy's investigations, she had become an actress. The only member of the team who hadn't lived under the same roof was the barrister, Angus Marshall. He presented their cases, often pro bono, once the evidence for a client had been collected and verified.

"I couldn't think of a better way to spend the day." He lowered his voice. "Have we heard any more of The Vicar?"

Paddy shook his head and combed his thick fingers through his still vibrant red hair. His blue eyes narrowed in disgust. "The man's like fog. He just dissipates 'fore ye can catch him. Word has it he's left Town for a while. But his time is comin'. I feel it in my bones."

"Even the slipperiest of eels eventually make their way to the trap." Sampson laughed, remembering when he first heard that saying. He and Gus had been taking biscuits from the kitchen, and one day, Maggie had lain in wait. The wooden spoon she'd rapped on their hands had certainly felt like a trap.

Sam thought about Mrs. Brown as he walked home. Perhaps he'd stop by St. James's Park next Sunday before going to the O'Briens. His family had a passion for sweets, and that delightful costermonger had a passion for making them. He could provide Maggie with a birthday treat and give some business to a hardworking woman. What would be the harm?

As he took the steps to his rented quarters, a smile curved his lips, and his heart beat a little faster.

* * *

Two days later

"Well, Dr. Brooks, what did you find?" asked Walters. "Drowning, or no?"

They were in the back room of the Dog's Bone. Ben had come along with Sam since they were taking in a play later at Vauxhall.

"Your instincts—and the landlady's—were correct," Sam informed Harry. "The man didn't drown—unless someone followed him into the Thames and then stabbed him repeatedly underwater." He paused, remembering the gruesome sight under the dead man's clothes. "He was wearing a good quality wool coat in August, which I would assume was supposed to soak up the blood while they transported him to the river. The bruises all over his body, and the differences in color among them, indicate he may have been tortured for some time before being dumped."

Walters snorted. "That's what I needed to know. I'll start with who he was seen with last. I wonder if they got the information they wanted—or didn't want him talking. Mayhap an interrogation gone wrong."

"If anyone can find the truth, it's you, Brother," said Benjamin. "But if you decide to search his home, please don't tell me. Unless you are caught, then of course I will be there." Humor sparked in his light-brown eyes.

"Won't be the first time," Walters agreed with a grin. "If he was working for The Vicar, I doubt anyone will miss him. Or stick their neck out to talk to you." Sampson knew his

words sounded cold, but the man *had* been a criminal, working with two of the men who had sent his parents to debtors' prison.

"True. His wife was robbed and killed not too long ago, according to the tavern keeper on the corner." Harry rubbed his jaw. "Sounds like a lot of bad luck in a short period of time."

"Coincidence?" asked Ben, a doubtful look on his face.

"You know what Paddy says." Guilt enveloped Sam now, thinking of the dead man's wife. It was wrong to judge a man, not knowing his circumstances.

"There are no coincidences," the three said in unison.

CHAPTER 4

$\mathcal{D}$ ottie packed up her cart and headed home. It had been a long week, but having Violet waiting for her lightened her heart. She wasn't speaking yet, but Dottie had a hunch she would. The child had nodded when asked if she'd ever talked. So, something had happened. The girl's brown eyes had shone with tears when she nodded again. They'd left the subject alone after that.

When she entered the kitchen, Violet looked up from the dishes she was scrubbing. She set down the pot and wiped her hands on the oversized apron that Mrs. Clatterly had given her, then ran to Dottie, and threw her arms around her.

"I missed you too, sweeting," she said, kissing the top of the girl's head. "Keeping busy?"

The girl nodded and pointed to the sink, going back to finish the pans.

Mrs. Clatterly bustled in. "She's a little angel, she is. The darling snuck into the public room and began clearing dishes from the table. Didn't ask her to do a thing, just wanted to help." The older woman blew at a strand of brown hair streaked with gray, then tucked it under her mobcap. Her usual pink cheeks were red, and she dabbed at the sweat on her brow with her apron. "I'll hate to see her leave. We've never been blessed with one of our own, and I enjoy having a young one under foot."

That was a relief since Dottie wasn't letting the girl go anywhere. Unless they actually found a family member, of course. "It's a brutal heat today. I'll unpack my cart and help you. I've got six pasties left."

They had begun selling anything remaining on her cart to the patrons at the tavern, splitting the profit. The customers were happy with the occasional treat, Dottie didn't lose any money, and the Clatterlys had another reason to be satisfied with their arrangement.

"Mr. Wells will be happy to hear that. He's disappointed when you sell out." Mrs. Clatterly bustled out, calling over her shoulder, "If you can heat up more stew, I'd be thankful. Mr. Clatterly is doing better but still moving slow. It took him almost a quarter of an hour to hobble down the stairs this morning. I can't spend as much time in the kitchen as I'd like."

Later that evening, Dottie and Violet sat in front of the small coal stove. Dottie rocked as she sewed, and Violet sprawled out on her stomach on the faded thick carpet. She turned the pages of *Tom Thumb's Pretty Song Book*, Dottie's cherished children's book, giggling occasionally at the illustrations or pointing at something in a silent question to Dottie.

"Are you happy here, sweeting?" she asked the child.

Violet nodded, her smile slipping as fear crept into her brown eyes.

"No, I haven't any intention of sending you away. You are

welcome as long as you're happy." She put her mending on her lap. "Do you know if you have any other family?"

The girl shook her head.

"You had a brother. And a father. Did you know your mother?"

A quick nod of her head, and the child quickly looked back at the book.

Dottie realized it was probably a sad tale. "Well if you do want to stay, you'll have to begin lessons."

Violet gave her a questioning look.

"There are printed words on those pages that you could read. They will tell you the story better than the illustrations and add to the meaning of the pictures. Some of them are songs we could sing together."

Understanding lit up Violet's eyes, and she nodded.

"Without speech, it will be more difficult, but we'll manage. I was a teacher before I married." She sighed and smiled down on her daught—

She's not your child.

Dottie watched Violet, her flaxen locks trailing the pages, her eyes searching between the illustrations and the words with renewed interest.

But she could be.

Dottie had become attached to the child in such a short time. Fate had crossed their paths for a reason. She believed that with all her heart. Perhaps even the horror of Robert had led her to this purpose. Dottie spoke her mind, said her thoughts out loud now because someone was there to listen. She also began singing again while she worked and had been silently thrilled when Violet had hummed along this morning.

The pair had quickly fallen into an evening routine. First, they would finish chores with Mrs. Clatterly in the kitchen, then retire to their room. There, they would count the money she'd made that day—Violet separated the coins into piles by size while Dottie counted, then added the total to her ledger. When there was a large enough pile, Mrs. Clatterly would take the silver and copper to the bank for larger coins. Finally, they ate a light supper together before sitting in front of the small stove. Dottie had always ended her evenings before a hearth. The stove was not lit, of course, since they had no need of heat this time of year. But the habit gave her a feeling of security, going through the motions of a schedule she'd followed for so many years. She hoped it would do the same for Violet.

"We'll start with your name. Everyone should be able to sign their own name," she told Violet.

The next day was Sunday. Mrs. Clatterly came into the kitchen as Dottie wrapped the pastries for St. James's. "Oh, ma'am, I wanted to thank you for Violet's shoes. I hoped to get her a new pair next week. I'll settle up with you when I return this evening."

The landlady waved a hand at her. "Absolutely not. The lass has been working hard, and we ain't no workhouse here. She's earning those shoes, she is."

Dottie's eyes burned with emotion. "You are too kind, ma'am. I appreciate it. We both do!"

"Now be gone or you won't get a good spot. The heat's finally let up, so them highborn folks won't all be flockin' to Gunter's or Farrance's for ices today." Mrs. Clatterly smiled at Violet. "Well, my girl, let's get Mr. Clatterly something to eat. He's grumpy as a bear when his stomach is empty."

Humming a bawdy tune she'd heard the other night in the tavern, Dottie made her way along Friday Street, wrinkling her nose at the briny scent of fish, and turned left onto Cheap Street. It was a beautiful sunny day with a slight breeze, and she made the walk in less than an hour. It was early for anyone to be on the promenade yet, but she'd wanted to be close to the main entrance. She settled on her stool and began to read the book she'd brought along, but her mind kept wandering to the gentleman she'd met last week.

Dr. Sampson Brooks. A physician.

"Good day, Mrs. Brown," a deep male voice said, interrupting her daydreaming.

She looked up to see the man of her thoughts smiling at her and inspecting her pastries. "Good day to you, Dr. Brooks," she replied with a warm smile.

"You remember my name? I'm impressed."

"As you remembered mine. I, too, am impressed." Her cheeks heated, and she silently scolded herself. She was too old to be acting like a young miss. Love and romance were in the past for her.

"I've a party to go to this evening and thought to bring some of your delicious goods with me. What have we today?" He looked very handsome in his beaver hat, deep-blue riding coat, and shining Hoby boots. As he moved his head to look at the pastries, the sun brought out golden streaks in his brown hair.

"No tarts today, I'm sorry to say. But I have Shrewsbury biscuits and rout cakes," she said, pointing and realizing she still had the book in her hand.

At Dr. Brooks's look of surprise, she quickly set it on her stool. "The currants in the rout cakes are fresh and plump."

He shook his head. "What are you reading?"

"The Romance of the Forest by—"

"Ann Radcliffe. Yes, I've read about the mysterious de la Motte family." There was a question in his gaze, and she knew he wondered how a costermonger would happen to have a novel. "Do you enjoy reading?"

"I do. I was an instructor at the Darlington School for Girls before I married." His hazel eyes, brimming with curiosity, had more gold flecks than she remembered. "I'm surprised *you* would have read such a novel."

"Gothic? As a boy, I read anything. I still would if I had the time. What subjects did you teach?" He crossed his arms, giving her his full attention. The sleeves of his riding coat stretched across muscled arms.

She directed her gaze back to his face. His very handsome face. "French—"

"French?"

His astonished tone irked her just a bit. "Yes, French and the pianoforte, and skills for running a household. Budgets and meal planning." She sniffed. "You're surprised."

"Stunned as a matter of fact." He grinned, showing his dimples. "Beautiful and intelligent. A rare combination."

"Especially pushing a pastry cart?" She grinned back. His jocular mood was infectious. Who was she to take umbrage? The widow of a criminal, no less.

"Exactly! Pardon my shock, although now you'll have to put up with a discussion of the novel when you finish it." He rubbed his chin. "Do you enjoy poetry?"

She shrugged. "Some. And you?"

"Despise it," he said in mock horror. "I remember trying to write a poem for a girl that I was arsey varsey over. The rhyming was absolutely horrid."

Dottie laughed. "How old were you?"

"Fourteen and very, very awkward."

"I can't imagine you as awkward, sir." She bit her lip as she realized he was flirting with her—and she was reciprocating. While flattered, she didn't have the time or inclination for coquetry. Dottie was determined never to succumb again to a man's sweet-talk. A hard lesson learned in her short life.

"My fourteen-year-old self thanks you." He chuckled and returned his attention to her cart. "Let's see, there will be..."

His fingers flicked as he mentally counted. "I suppose there might be as many as a dozen. Since I'm not sure what everyone would prefer, why don't I take a dozen of each?"

Dottie gasped. That would be over half her inventory for the day. She could be home early, perhaps take Violet out for tea. "My goodness. Are you sure?"

"Yes, I don't want to be responsible for someone not getting their favorite. It's a birthday party, after all." He fished in his pocket for some coins.

"Someone special, I assume?" She wanted to know if he was married—no, she didn't. Yes, she did. Dottie told herself it was only so she would know if he was being kind or hoping for something in return for such generosity.

"I'd say very special. The couple saved me from freezing to death in the street and put me through school. It's her celebration." He watched her for a reaction.

"You're an orphan?" This was a surprise.

"No, well, yes." He shook his head. "Both my parents are dead, yes, but they were alive when I was a child. Still, the O'Briens helped raise me into the man I am today." The softness in his hazel eyes told her how much he cared for this couple. "They saved me from a life I was ill-suited for."

"It sounds like an interesting tale." He had piqued her curiosity.

"And one for another day when I have more time." He handed her several coins, waved away her protestations, and collected his treats wrapped in newspaper and tied with a string. "Enjoy this lovely day, Mrs. Brown."

So he meant to stop again? Heat spread up her neck. He tipped his hat and picked up the bundle, dipping a finger under the string. His dimples deepened, causing butterflies to swarm in her stomach. With such a reaction every time she saw the man, Dottie wasn't sure if she hoped he returned or stayed away. Goodness, she felt like a schoolgirl.

"Enjoy your party, Dr. Brooks," she called out belatedly, watching him walk away to collect his horse from the boy holding his reins. The lad's eyes opened wide at the coin given him. It seemed the physician was a charitable man, along with having good looks and a fine profession.

But the worst of men could appear to be the best of men.

CHAPTER 5

$\mathcal{A}$s Sam rode back to Cheapside, crossing over to the north side and the wealthier homes, a plan began to take shape. He liked Mrs. Brown. Yes, he was also attracted to her. She was a beauty. But he *liked* her. There was kindness mixed with the pain in her deep-blue eyes. Perhaps next week, he'd find out about the girl who had been with her at the hanging. Daughter? Sister? But the child's appearance, filthy and unkempt, had been a direct contrast to the lovely Mrs. Brown. A waif she'd found? He could sympathize with that. Then again, she could be a tomboy, refusing to stay clean, longing for the freedom of a boy. Memories of a ragtag Nora sprang to mind, her red hair a frizzy lump on her head, dress torn, boots muddy while she tried to keep up with her brothers.

So, the pastry lady had worked at a girls' school. Sampson was on the board for the Magdalen House, a hospital established in 1758 to take in "penitent prostitutes and young women" who had been seduced or shunned and might be forced into prostitution. It was a worthy charity, and he was proud to be a part of it. The staff worked to reunite the upper-class women with their families, and those who couldn't return home were taught working skills. No woman was forced out until she found a good position and could support herself.

But the charity did not take in pregnant women. Sam had seen girls as young as thirteen turned away, swollen with child. He hated the terrified look in their eyes, knowing what they faced. For the past few months, he'd been thinking about opening a hospital for these unfortunates. And now, he wondered if Mrs. Brown could be part of his scheme. He still had to organize wealthy benefactors, find a suitable building, and create a budget. For now, the educated costermonger was another pearl forming in the back of his mind.

Leaving Jack at a nearby mews, Sam walked down the block to the O'Briens' townhouse. The door opened, raucous laughter spilling out the door.

"Sampson! C'mere, boyo," boomed a voice from behind the housekeeper. "We've been waitin' for ye."

The parlor was crowded with the "family" all in one room. There were his brothers-by-choice, including Walters. The six men were of various heights and builds, men he'd known since he or they had been lost boys on the streets. Sitting next to Mrs. O'Brien was Honora, the last orphan to enter the Irishman's fold, coming to them as a foundling. With so many "brothers," the lass had been spoiled rotten.

Honora was now going on twenty, a young woman with bright red hair and green eyes who could truly pass as one of the O'Briens' natural offspring. She was tough as old leather but lovely to look at, could mimic any brogue, and was proficient at disguise. The female counterpart to Walters. She was also making a name for herself on stage as Nora Diamond. The girl was fearless and had been vital in tracking down key figures in the last several cases.

All of them were talking at once, asking how the others

had been, when a shrill whistle froze every tongue. "Wind yer necks in and let me speak!" yelled Margaret O'Brien. "Now c'mere to me."

A mumbled chorus of "Sure now" and "Sorry" echoed against the paneled walls of the parlor.

They all obeyed as they had since they were children and gathered around her rocker near the hearth. Seven pairs of feet trampled the worn forest-green Wilton carpet as they waited for the matriarch to speak. Margaret's auburn hair shone with bits of silver, her dark eyes glittering as she gazed at each of them. "My boys," she said with a weepy smile. "I love ye all. And *we've* an announcement to make." She stared pointedly at Honora.

"Uh, yes," agreed Honora hesitantly. "I have decided to give up my stealthy ways and focus my energy on stage."

Silence.

"Sure, look," said Paddy to fill the awkward moment. "We knew she'd marry some day and leave us. Consider dis as marryin' da theater."

"Congratulations." Clayton came forward first. With his reddish-brown hair and green eyes, he was the only one who might have passed as Honora's brother. He'd been taken in by Mrs. O'Brien at the age of nine, when his mother died. Never knowing his father, Clayton would have ended up on the streets. "I'll rent a box for the season."

Honora laughed. "You don't even know where I'll be performing yet."

"But we'll be there," added Eli, the youngest detective of the group.

"Wouldn't miss it," agreed Benjamin, their solicitor, light-brown eyes merry beneath a mass of blond curls.

Gus, a massive man with straight dark hair always pulled back at the neck and fastened with a leather tie, grinned down at her. "If you need a bodyguard, I'm happy to slap a few heads together. They'll be fightin' for a pretty thing like you. All those oglin' men and jealous wives." It was a badly kept secret that Gus had a tendre for Honora.

"Thank you, August," Honora said with a sweet smile, rising to give him a kiss on the cheek. "I know you'll always be here for me."

Angus Marshall, the barrister, cleared his throat. "I may not have been raised under this roof as all of you have, but I feel as though you are all kin." Angus raised his glass of brandy. "To Nora Diamond, may she have a bright and promising future."

"Aye" and "Here, here" and "To be sure" mixed together at once to wish one of their own a happy life.

"Now." Paddy raised his glass again. "To da finest o' women, da flower of da flock! My Margaret, my love."

They all raised their voices and toasted the woman who meant so much to them. She'd fed them, bathed them, doctored their fevers and broken bones, and loved them.

Sir Harry Walters raised his glass. "To the dear woman who chased the meanness out of each of us when it dared to show its face. You showed us kindness when the world was cruel and taught us that compassion can still be found in those around us."

"Sounds like being affianced has put silver on his tongue," Gus said with a chuckle. "Where is the soon-to-be Lady Walters?"

"Unfortunately, she had a previous engagement and begs me to send her warmest regards." Walters grimaced. "A musicale I was able to escape, rescued by Margaret. Again."

After a splendid dinner of clear broth, oysters that were back in season and fresh pork, late peas, and sliced cucumbers, they enjoyed a plate of nuts, cheeses, and the Shrewsbury biscuits and rout cakes with fruit preserves. The conversation was lively, with someone always talking over someone else, stopping, apologizing, and then starting all over again.

This was where Sampson felt at home, needed and loved, a part of this pieced-together brood who would give their lives for one another. He wondered where he might have ended up without the O'Briens. Without the advice of Walters or his best friend Benjamin or the loyalty of them all. While he longed for his parents, especially during Christmastide, he was the luckiest of men to be part of this loving household.

Besides the camaraderie, they all had a bond, a shared purpose working for Paddy. Finding criminals, helping victims, and bringing justice to those who had been wronged. It was a heavy responsibility when they took on a case, whether it was for an individual or the Crown, and one they each took seriously. Pride was a funny thing: It could pull a man up from the gutter one day and strike him down the next.

Margaret sat next to him as everyone moved from the dining room back to the parlor, her plump hands smoothing out her skirts. There would be singing and dancing, more spirits, more laughter. "Before we go, tell me where ye bought those fine cakes and biscuits. I expected yer usual bottle o' Irish whiskey."

"Ah, but it's your day not Paddy's. I don't think the whiskey would have been to your liking." He kissed her cheek. "Has it been a fine afternoon?"

"'Tis been a grand day. How can it not be with my family about me?"

Paddy and Margaret had never been blessed with children of their own. They threw themselves wholeheartedly into the family they had created. Sam couldn't have been more cherished by his own parents.

"There's a pretty little costermonger near St. James's Park on Sundays. Last week, she had the tastiest berry tarts."

"Yer favorite," Margaret added with a smile. "A pretty little t'ing, is she? Sounds like yer takin' dis new idea of a wife to heart. Unmarried or widowed?"

He gave her a side-look and shook his head. "A widow, but don't get any ideas. While I have decided on the need to marry, there is no one in particular who has caught my interest yet."

"Me, ideas?" she asked, a twinkle in her dark eyes. "I only want ye happy."

"Your mission has been accomplished." Sam knew this was true for all of them. The O'Briens had saved their lives. "She had a book with her, which is very unusual for someone working a cart. She intrigued me. That's all. I barely know her."

"Ah, sorry, but yer eyes tell a different story. The heart has no calendar or clock." She patted his hand. "A mother always knows. Won't ye unburden yer mind?"

With a sigh, Sam realized he wanted to. The woman always knew when he had something worrying him. So, he told her about the last admission day at Magdalen House and the poor girl who had been turned away. How he hoped to open something similar but for those who found themselves alone *and* with child.

"'Tis more dan a dream, ain't it, Sampson? Ye already have some bits of a plan in place." She beamed at him, her cheeks round as her smile grew. "And how does da pretty little costermonger fit in?"

"She taught at a girls' school—" Sometimes he swore this woman was a seer from the days of old. Was it intuition? Would he have the same kind of intuition with his own offspring? He doubted it.

"Go on."

With a resigned sigh, he explained the rest of his scheme to procure a building with his own funds, then look for benefactors to help run the home. "And Mrs. Brown might be the perfect instructor to teach these girls skills that will help them become independent, give them the ability to raise their children without…"

"Becomin' doxies," Margaret finished.

"Precisely," he agreed, a bit embarrassed.

"'Tis a fine goal, Sampson. If anyone can accomplish it, 'tis you."

"As Paddy says, all your geese are swans."

"Nothin' wrong with swans." She patted his hand and rose to join the others. "When ye decide to court dis pastry woman, remember to bring her home for us to meet."

She walked away before he could respond, leaving him astonished at her insight as he followed her to the parlor. The woman had a gift. If he could bottle and sell it, the Hospital of Hope would be up and running in no time.

CHAPTER 6

End of October

It was Sunday. Dottie packed her cart, looked at the dreary day, and debated going to St. James's. If it didn't clear up, there would be no one to sell her goods to. But Dr. Brooks might appear, as he had each week since their first meeting. He never stayed overly long, but bought half her pastries, saying he was now expected to bring something for his Sunday dinners. Whether that was true, she didn't know. But selling out so quickly gave her extra time with Violet.

"Close the O on your name, Violet, or it will look like a U. Then we'll have to pronounce your name Vi*oo*let."

The girl giggled at that and shook her head. But she wiped the offending O from the writing slate and made another. She looked up at Dottie for approval.

"Very nice," she said and kissed the child on top of her head. Humming and giggling had become such a sweet sound. But would she ever hear actual words coming from the girl's mouth? "Now, let's try your numbers 1 through 5. I'll write them first, and you will copy them."

Violet nodded, her tongue peeking out as she concentrated on forming the numbers. She was a curious student and learned quickly. It filled a void in Dottie to be teaching again. She hadn't realized how much she had missed it.

She peered out the window. "I hope it stops raining."

Violet spread out her hands and put her thumbs together, moving back and forth like a ship, then pointed to the Bible they read from each night.

"Oh my," Dottie said with a chuckle, "I hope we don't need to build an ark."

Violet nodded enthusiastically.

She went behind the stove, careful of the hot metal from the glowing coal, and retrieved the tin that held her savings. Taking out all the ha'pennies, she pushed them toward Violet. "Remember how to count along with the numbers?"

The little girl nodded, placing one penny below her newly scratched numeral *1*, then two pennies under her scrawled *2*, and continued until there were five coins lined up beneath the *5*.

"Very good!" Dottie pointed at the board, explaining the pattern of "one more" in each row. Then she lined ten of the pennies in front of the girl and began to count. Violet followed along with her, touching each coin as Dottie said the number.

When the lesson was over, Dottie put the coins back in the tin and shook it, scowling at the contents. "I'll be old and gray by the time I make enough money to take us to America."

Violet gasped and pointed to herself, questioning if Dottie meant to take her.

"Of course, dear girl, as long as you want to go."

Violet nodded, a huge grin on her face.

"We can start over. I'll be a widow, you're my daughter, and we're searching for relations. I don't have any that I know of, but it's a good tale as to why we left England." If she'd had references, Dottie could have tried for a position of cook if one for governess or instructor hadn't worked out. Across the ocean lay a world full of possibilities. There was a myriad of excuses as to how she had "lost" her references on the voyage over. She could earn a decent wage and be a proper mother to her "daughter."

Violet jumped up, rounded the table, and threw her arms around Dottie. The hug was so powerful, it almost knocked Dottie off the chair. She wrapped her arms around the child, burying her face in the soft blonde waves. This could be enough for her. They could be happy, the two of them together.

Just as suddenly, Violet placed a kiss on Dottie's cheek and ran into the kitchen.

With a sigh, she rose and replaced the tin. A weak ray of sunshine peeked through the curtains. It looked like she'd be going to St. James's Park after all. Her stomach did a slight flip.

She had given up trying to curb the attraction she felt toward Dr. Brooks. What was the harm? He was a handsome man who treated her nicely, proving to be her best customer in fact. A little flirting made her feel young again and helped pass the time. He never acted untoward, and she didn't dream of such a man wanting anything more serious than a light flirtation every Sunday. He had mentioned Violet several times, calling her Dottie's daughter. Dottie had given him Violet's name but hadn't corrected him on the child's family. What was the harm?

The temperatures had dropped, a definite chill seeping through the city. Winter was making itself known, and

Dottie was grateful for the brown wool redingote. By the time she was settled outside the park, her cheeks were cold. As long as her nose didn't run…

"Good afternoon, Mrs. Brown. I wasn't sure if the weather was going to cooperate today."

There he was, dressed in a forest-green riding coat that brought out the green in his hazel eyes. Fawn-colored breeches hugged hard thighs that disappeared into shining black boots. When he removed his hat, his hair had lost the sun-touched streaks and was more umber with slight curls brushing his collar. It made him seem older, more serious. Until the creases in his cheeks deepened, and he grinned at her with a bow. My, but he was handsome.

"Good day to you, sir." She stood, setting her book on the stool. "Have you been well?"

"Excellent, and you?"

"Happy to have another fine day to sell you some pastries." With a smile, she pulled back a cloth. "Apple tarts for a certain physician who has a preference for them."

A hand went to his chest. "Oh, you've stolen my heart through my stomach." He went to pick one up, and Dottie slapped his hand.

"Oh," she cried, mortified at her action. She was accustomed to fending off Violet and Mr. Clatterly while she baked. "I forget myself. My apologies." Heat rose up her neck and flooded her cheeks. What would he think?

Laughter erupted from him, his eyes twinkling as he shook his hand. "You wound me, Mrs. Brown. There's a vixen hiding beneath your gentle exterior."

"I don't know what I was thinking… why I would…" Her words faded as she realized he was staring at her mouth. It made her do the same. That was a mistake. Wondering what those full lips would feel like against hers sent her stomach tumbling.

"Mrs. Brown, may I speak plainly?"

Had she put him off with her behavior? Lost her best customer? She could only answer with a nod.

"We've been meeting for the past eight weeks, exchanging pleasantries and pastries. Very enjoyable, I admit, but I'd like to see you without the cart between us." He paused, his gaze direct and penetrating, warm and knowing, as if he could see her quivering inside.

"I-I don't know... I-this is unexpected." She chewed her bottom lip. "You and I are from different worlds, I believe. I'm not—"

"You are a lovely, educated woman who has a talent for baking. I am the son of a bookshop owner who ended up in debtors' prison for years. We are not so far apart that we cannot socialize." He paused as if making a decision. "A carriage ride or a cup of tea? We can share our stories, then you may decide if we are suited to continue a friendship."

How did she respond to that? He was right, of course. Her own father had been a steward for an earl. His position had come with certain privileges. No one would comment on a steward's daughter stepping out with a physician. Except she was a costermonger now. Not someone's daughter or an instructor.

"Is it propriety? I assumed from your attire that you were no longer in mourning. If you are not yet ready for an outing, I understand and apologize." Yet his eyes pleaded with her, his smile tempting her to say yes. "Our brief conversations have been delightful. I hope to have lengthier discussions at our leisure and get to know you better. I have a feeling you may have quite a story behind those sparkling blue eyes."

Dottie heard herself say, "I would be honored to have tea with you, Dr. Brooks. There's no need for flummery."

"A sincere compliment."

She nodded, watching a lopsided smile curve his mouth before he said, "Excellent. Now, about those tarts. I believe I'll take the lot."

"All of them?" She chuckled. "You can't possibly eat everything you purchase."

"No, no. I am on the board of Magdalen House and bring whatever is left to our weekly meetings." He winked at her. "You've made me quite popular."

How could she say *no* to this man? Kind, intelligent, generous, and good-looking. Well, she could enjoy his company without unlocking her heart. Details of her past could be kept vague. Besides, with winter on their heels, it was good to know a doctor.

"I've heard of the hospital. Do you provide medical services for the women there?"

"I do. I was impressed with the mission of Magdalen and the work they've done for females who have been taken advantage of or cast out. No person should be alone. I understand what desperation feels like and wish it on no one."

"As do I. You are a good man." And he was. Too good for her.

"I endeavor to make my parents proud every day. And I hope they look down on me and approve."

"I'm sure they do, Dr. Brooks." She handed him the tarts. This time, both his hands cradled hers as he took the bundle. Warmth spread through her like a cheery hearth fire.

"Shall we set a date?" he asked, his thick brows wiggling. "Is there a time that is better for you? Perhaps when you have finished your day?"

Dottie told him the direction on Watling Street, and they arranged to have tea in the Clatterly public room the next Wednesday afternoon. Though a widow, she wasn't comfortable meeting a man alone. With her landlord's hawk-like gaze on them, Dottie could relax.

"You have given me something to look forward to, Mrs. Brown. Until Wednesday."

She watched him walk away, wondering at his motive. Surely, there was no lack of ladies vying for his attention. Would the kind physician still be interested when he learned her husband had died on the gallows? Yet, he had been there that day. She did not see him as a man who went to public executions for entertainment. Why *had* he attended?

CHAPTER 7

Wednesday

*S*ampson shook his head to clear it. *Ridiculous.* How could he be nervous? Yet his palms were sweaty, and he kept clearing his throat. The balding barkeep, with one foot propped up on a stool and a scowl on his ruddy face, continued to stare silently at him with menacing dark eyes after serving up an ale. Sam had quickly retreated to a table after asking for Mrs. Brown.

Mr. Clatterly, he presumed, was extremely protective for a landlord.

A plump woman with soft brown eyes bustled in with a tea tray. She set it down on Sam's table with a wide smile, then put her hands on her hips.

Mrs. Clatterly, he assumed again, was much friendlier than her husband. How had they known who he was? There were more than a dozen men in the place.

"I'm Mrs. Clatterly, and that beast of a man over there is my husband."

"It's a pleasure to meet you, ma'am. I'm Dr. Brooks," he said, standing for a proper introduction.

She eyed the ale he was sipping. "A bit of courage before she comes, eh? Well, best hurry. Dottie will be here in a blink."

They called her Dottie instead of Dorothea? Dottie Brown. It had a warm sound to it.

Then she was standing before him, no heavy coat or hat on her head.

"Mrs. Brown," he said simply, his discomfort evaporating at the sight of her.

He could drown in those ocean-blue eyes. Her thick auburn hair was pulled up in the back, long curls tickling her slender neck. A modest dress of dove gray clung to her full figure, taking his imagination for a jaunt. She looked every bit the lady who might instruct the daughters of wealthy merchants.

"Dr. Brooks," she replied with a nod of her head. She murmured her thanks as he held out her chair. "Did you find the place without much trouble?"

He nodded. "I grew up in Cheapside. And you?"

"My father was steward for the Earl of Langhorn's country estate in Kent. I lived there until I was fourteen." She held up the teapot, an eyebrow up in question. He nodded, pushed the bumper of ale away, and she poured them each a cup. "My mother died when I was four—a fever of some sort is all I remember. Papa didn't talk about it much. He loved her so."

"My parents were also dedicated to each other. I hope to have the same someday." Sam saw the panic in her eyes. "Not that I'm ready to wear the leg shackles quite yet."

He was rewarded with a brilliant smile as she visibly

relaxed. "Your father was obviously an educated man. Did he or your mother insist you were too?"

"Both my parents believed in the power of learning. Papa convinced his lordship to allow me to study with his daughter. There was no one else nearby that was close to her age. So, I received lessons and provided companionship in return."

"He sounds like an astute man. Living above a bookshop, I had knowledge at my fingertips." Sam remembered the place with fondness despite the sad ending.

"You are your only limitation, my father always said. I believed him when I was younger."

"You don't believe him now?" He wondered at the sorrow that darkened her eyes, the lines that creased the corners, telling him she'd also known pain.

"There are so many conditions and obstacles in this life that are out of one's hands. We can strive to become better, but we can only rise as far as the world, or society, will allow us." She shrugged. "Life has a way of reminding us that we are not always in control of our destiny."

So true. "Why did you leave the blissful fields of southern England at fourteen? School?"

"My father fell from his horse and broke his neck. My mother's family disowned her when she married Papa because he was a foundling. Mama was the sixth child of a baron, and my grandmother had hopes to aspire in society. So, I was alone, as far as relations, and in a peculiar position. Not a domestic, yet not one of the family." She hesitated, her gaze scanning the room, smiling at a customer, then studying her teacup. "So yes, I left to continue my education, though not according to the original plan. The earl had been close to my father, took pity on me, and sent me to a boarding school with a small allowance until I was of age."

"A generous lord."

"Very. I was befriended by an instructor at the academy, who planned to open her own school for girls, and she personally trained me. When I turned eighteen, she offered me a position at the Darlington School for Girls." A bitter-sweet smile curled her plump lips. "Mrs. Darlington is a fine, caring woman. I don't know what I might have done without the earl's generosity and her guidance."

"In my opinion, humble as it is, fate puts who we need in our path. We can accept the gift or turn away from it. Fortunately, it sounds like both of us accepted those who offered a lending hand." He studied her for a moment as she sipped her tea. "The puzzle begins to come together. You intrigued me from that first day at St. James's. A costermonger who spoke without a cockney accent, refined in her movements, and a smile that pulled me to your cart."

She blushed. "You made a fine figure yourself, sitting on your horse."

He wanted to ask her why she had been at the hanging. *That* had been the first time he'd noticed her. But something told him to wait, to learn more about her before bringing it up.

"Enough about me for now. How did you come to be a physician? What happened to your parents?" She fiddled with one of the curls at her pink cheek. "I'm sorry. If you don't care to talk about it, I understand."

"It's fine. I was a boy of ten, almost eleven, when my world turned upside down. My father, while a learned man, didn't have much common sense. Too much faith in his fellow man." He nodded as she offered him more tea. "A swindler of the worst kind sold him insurance for the book-shop. It cost a tidy sum but came with a certificate of guaran-tee. Father never suspected a thing until there was a fire in the shop, and he went to collect."

"There was no such insurance company?"

Sam shook his head with a derisive chuckle. "The man had rented an office space for the scheme and left after he collected enough fees. We were ruined. I stayed with them at King's Bench until my father's funds ran low. I realized I was another mouth to feed."

"What did you do?"

"Found work wherever I could, stole food when my stomach demanded I fill it, and gave anything I earned to my parents so they could eat. It still goes on, you know. Charging people for their stay in prison. How does one pay off a debt if they have to pay to survive in gaol?" He shrugged. "A wrong I shall never be able to right."

Mrs. Brown reached out, her hand covering his. "You were a brave boy." Her compassion was sincere, and without thinking, he covered her hand with his other. It seemed such a natural reaction to her concern.

"I was a desperate boy. I had no skills, but I was well-read and clever. It was then I realized there were two kinds of intelligence—academia and life lessons. I learned the latter rather quickly."

Mrs. Clatterly was serving a table next to them, and she looked over her shoulder, her eyes resting on their joined hands. "Do you need a fresh pot?"

Sam understood. Though Mrs. Brown was a widow, the landlady was determined to maintain propriety. He slid his hand back with a grin, and Mrs. Brown did the same, her cheeks adorably pink. How old was she? Early twenties, perhaps?

"No, thank you, ma'am. But it was delicious." He smiled when she beamed at the compliment. "I don't want to over-stay my welcome on the first visit."

"You plan to come see us again, do you?" Mrs. Clatterly's hip bumped Mrs. Brown's shoulder. The widow drew in a breath and shook her head ever so slightly at the older woman.

"If Mrs. Brown allows it, I would be honored to continue our conversation. May I?" Sam gave her his most persuasive smile, knowing his dimples were on full display. Women seemed to like the dents in his cheeks. He'd use them to his advantage if it got him more time with this captivating woman.

"I'll see you on Sunday, of course," she murmured. "Yes?"

"Unless the weather says otherwise."

She stood, and he did the same. "I suppose, if you're still interested on Sunday, we could arrange another time."

"If I must wait, I will. Until then, Mrs. Brown," Sam murmured, taking her hand and kissing the top of it. He had the strangest urge to trail kisses all the way up her arm. He dropped a coin on the table for the tea and ale and made his way to the door.

Despite all he'd learned about this woman—one he now admitted stirred his blood—his curiosity had been piqued rather than satisfied. How had she ended up in Cheapside? What happened to her husband? Where was her daughter? Sam was confident he'd discover her past and its secrets if he was patient. He was one of Paddy's Peelers, after all.

CHAPTER 8

*T*rue to his word, Dr. Brooks met her on Sunday and bought his usual bounty of pastries. They had agreed to repeat their tea on Wednesday. Dottie knew she shouldn't encourage him, but the man was so persuasive and such good company. On Tuesday, Mrs. Clatterly teased her about her "beau."

"He's a fine-looking gentleman, though Mr. Clatterly is reserving his opinion."

"As am I. In fact, I wonder why he's interested at all. I'm sure he would have no trouble courting a young miss from a good family." Why a widow with no social standing?

"You're still a lovely young woman. Why *wouldn't* he be interested?" Mrs. Clatterly poked Violet's belly. "What do you think of him?"

Violet frowned and shook her head, then ran to the sink and put on her apron. Dottie watched her thin shoulders shake as she scrubbed furiously at a pot. Was she jealous? They would discuss it later. The poor dear had enough sorrow in her life.

The following day, Dottie dressed carefully, telling herself it wasn't for Dr. Brooks. She wore a Devonshire brown walking dress, with the heart-shaped pendant her father had given her nestled above the square neckline. "Violet, how do I look?"

Violet grinned and nodded. Dottie had explained to her the previous night that, if it were in her power, nothing would ever part them. Knowing how life could change in a heartbeat, she couldn't promise the girl that it would *never* happen. No one could make any guarantees in this life. Dottie would never lie to the girl.

As she entered the public room, Mr. Wells waved to her from a table near the fireplace. She smiled and waved back. Several other patrons greeted her as she walked toward Dr. Brooks. He stood, smiling and handsome in pale trousers, a light-blue coat, and a white-and-blue striped waistcoat.

"Mrs. Brown, you look lovely." He bowed and took her hand before pulling back a chair. "I've ordered tea, and Mr. Clatterly is not scowling so harshly at me this week."

She laughed, her nervousness disappearing at his touch. "His bark is worse than his bite."

They discussed a variety of subjects, laughed, teased, and drank too much tea.

"May we meet again? Please don't make me wait until Sunday to say yes." He leaned forward as if about to share a secret. "I am not too proud to beg."

She chewed her bottom lip, watching pedestrians pass by the window and deliberating the wisdom of beginning such a friendship. "I suppose we could do this again."

"Would you consider an outing to Farrance's for tea? I will only keep you a respectable amount of time. Perhaps we could take a stroll in St. James's Park afterwards if the weather permits."

"That does sound tempting."

"We could enjoy a treat you didn't have to bake yourself."

"That might be nice. Yes, I accept. When?"

"Next Wednesday? And of course, I must see you on Sunday or the hospital board will be very disappointed." He rose when she did and took her hand. "Thank you for a wonderful afternoon."

* * *

Sampson snapped the reins, and the pair of gleaming chestnuts lunged forward into the traffic. He deftly handled the O'Briens' black-lacquered curricle, thinking he'd eventually need one of his own. The top was down—for now. It was a sunny day, and he was eager to be with Mrs. Brown without the Clatterlys or other patrons listening. He wanted to ask about her daughter, about her late husband, and how long she'd been widowed.

Most of all, he wanted her close beside him, elbows touching, smelling her scent as the breeze drifted his way. She smelled of citrus and cinnamon and cloves. He wanted to blow on those dangling auburn curls, jealous of them as they caressed her neck. Sink back into the velvet squab and study her profile, the delicate ears, the straight nose, the perfect chin, and the long lashes. For the third time in a week, he had dreamt of her—walking along the canal at St. James's, strolling along a beach in Brighton, dancing at a ball. Each time it ended with a kiss. Would he be disappointed? For he fully intended to kiss her today. If he had to put the top up and throw his greatcoat over them, their lips would meet.

He grinned as he turned onto Watling Street and slowed the pair in front of the Clatterlys. A lad ran up to take the harness, remembering Brooks from the past two weeks. "Ye can count on me, my lord," the boy said with a nod, a cocky slant to his shoulders. "I'm yer man."

With difficulty, Sam hid his smile and tossed the boy a coin. Entering the tavern, he peered around the room until his eyes adjusted from the bright sunlight. The hearth to the right crackled, several men sat in a back corner arguing good-naturedly over something, and the ever-so-congenial Mr. Clatterly sat with his arms crossed, only a slight scowl today.

A small girl with wild blonde curls escaping a too-big mobcap came from the kitchen, walked behind the bar, and tugged on Clatterly's waistcoat. To Sam's surprise, a delighted smile transformed the man's face. It was amazing—or the child was, for the barkeep looked like a different person.

The lass caught Sam staring at her. The brown eyes widened, and she turned and dashed back to the kitchen. As soon as she disappeared, Mrs. Brown came out, wearing the same gray dress from their first tea with a small hat perched on her head. He wondered if he'd be able to breathe if he saw her in a ball gown. Mrs. Clatterly helped her on with her brown redingote.

"Dr. Brooks, how good to see you again." She smiled, then waved to the men at the table, who paused in their argument to wave in return.

Sam bowed, and she took his arm, a beaming Mrs. Clatterly behind them, the little blonde hiding behind the older woman's skirts. He swore the girl frowned at him with the exact scowl the barkeep always wore. If she were the same girl he'd seen at the hanging, it was a miraculous change in appearance.

After helping Mrs. Brown up and into the curricle, he maneuvered the chestnut geldings around other carriages, hackneys, carts, and pedestrians. Cheapside Street was hectic, even in midafternoon, with businesses crammed along the busy thoroughfare. Sam would never understand the lure of the overpriced and limited shopping on Bond Street compared to this industrious area.

"So, tell me more about Dr. Brooks the urchin and how he pulled himself from the streets as a child." There was a good-natured smirk on her plump lips, and he wanted to kiss it off.

"Ah, the urchin, Sam."

"Sam?"

"My given name is Sampson. Sampson J. Brooks, but I'm also known as Sam by family and friends." He clicked to the horses after pausing for an elderly pedestrian. "I tried to steal a cane from the wrong man—or the right one, depending on how you look at it—on Christmas Eve. I had only stolen food before, but I was so cold and hungry. All I'd earned went to my parents, as I've said, and my mother was doing poorly."

"Oh, my. It must have been terrible." Her hand went to his forearm, and he didn't want her to remove it.

"It was. But Paddy saw something in me. Instead of calling the constable, he took me home. There was one other boy they had taken in—Harry Walters—and we became fast friends." He sighed, remembering that long ago night. "Because of the O'Briens, I was able to continue the path my father would have wanted, though I turned a different direction when I reached a fork."

"How's that?"

"I always thought I'd be a solicitor. It had been my and my father's plan. But after seeing so many sick in the prison and on the streets… I felt I could be of more service by practicing medicine." Did he sound too trite? He hoped not, though his goals did seem lofty even to himself at times.

"I'm glad you did. It suits you."

"Thanks to the O'Briens, I was able to attend university and, in my own way, help the family business."

"They sound like special people."

"Few could surpass them." He told her of the Peelers and the part he played to help his "second" family. "I found the books I pored through on plants and healing held my attention much more than dry legal cases. Maggie, Mrs. O'Brien, urged me to consider medicine, explaining my compassion for the sick and helpless would suit better for a doctor rather than a solicitor. She was right, of course, and here I am."

"I'm glad. You're a good man, and London needs them." She returned her hand to her lap and watched the passersby as they made their way to the confectioner's shop.

"Have you had a prosperous week so far, Mrs. Brown?" he asked, anxious to fill the silence.

"Yes, I've begun filling orders for Christmas pudding. Mr. Clatterly has been spreading the word to the patrons. He's such a dear."

Sam snorted. "Not to me. However, I did see a genuine smile on his face when a young girl pulled on his waistcoat." He gave her a side-look, hoping she'd indulge his curiosity.

"That's Violet. I do believe she's charmed him without a word."

"That's hard to believe. Does she get her charm from her mother?" he asked, probing again.

Mrs. Brown shook her head. "I have no idea. Violet doesn't speak of her, and her father is dead. We crossed paths, two females alone in London, and joined forces so to speak."

The girl wasn't her daughter? It made more sense. The woman he'd come to know would have spoken of the lass more if the lass had been her daughter. Was she the child he'd seen with Mrs. Brown that gruesome day? "It seems you have something common with the O'Briens."

Sam pulled up on the reins and slowed the horses as they came up to the corner of Spring Gardens and Cockspur Street. He jumped down from the curricle and came around to help Mrs. Brown. As she put her foot on the step and reached out for his shoulders, her half boot slipped. He caught her waist with both hands, lifting her and safely bringing her to the ground. Their bodies touched as he lowered her to her feet, and heat rushed from his chest through his core.

Stifling a moan, he asked, "Are you hurt?"

She shook her head but looked flushed. "N-no. Only my pride. I'm afraid I've never had an abundance of grace."

"I'm happy to catch you in my arms any time." Her smile made his pulse race. He held out his arm, and she took it as they entered Farrance's.

"Oh my, it smells divine in here," she gasped, closing her eyes and drawing in a deep breath. "Thank you for suggesting this."

They sat at a small table. A man came up and took their order of tea and a plate of various comfits and pastries.

"This tea is superb," she exclaimed. "And these cakes… I'm trying to determine what is in them. I must try to replicate them." Her face was flushed from the steaming tea, her eyes sparkling as she tried another candied fruit. "Are you not enjoying the sweets?"

"Indeed, I am," said Sam, placing his chin on his fist and smiling at her.

"Flummery, Dr. Brooks, but I enjoy it all the same," she said around a mouthful, then giggled.

"Please, call me Sampson… or Sam." He poured them more tea. "Unless you don't wish to continue our friendship, which would devastate me."

"Well, Sampson, we can't have that." She paused, her gaze holding his, and something changed between them at that moment.

It happened in a breath, but he knew she was finally giving in. Would give him a chance. His heart soared.

"Then you must call me Dorothea… or Dottie," she said at length. The tip of her tongue peeked out to swipe up a crumb at the corner of her mouth. His breath caught.

When they finished their tea and sweets, she wrapped up the last remaining candied fruit and tucked it in her reticule, murmuring, "For Violet." Then they made their way to St. James's Park.

It wasn't busy, being Wednesday, which Sam preferred. They strolled, her arm in his, and he thought they looked the perfect couple. Others passed them, smiled, and nodded as the pair spoke of books and music. They walked along the canal, and he told her of the pelicans residing there since Charles II. They talked of their favorite colors and smells and animals. The sun was setting when they made their way back to the curricle, and he hated for their time together to end.

Sam was happy with the day, felt he'd made progress with… Dottie. He liked the feel of her name on his tongue. That thought sent him in another direction, soft lips and…

He maneuvered her behind a cluster of trees, placing his hands on her arms. There were few people about, and they were in shadow. "Forgive me if this offends you, but I've wanted to kiss you for weeks. May I?" He waited, thinking he'd gone too far, when her blue eyes darkened. With desire? Did she feel the same?

"Yes, but—"

He couldn't wait and stepped closer, breathing in her sweet scent. Orange and cloves. She moved back, leaning against a tree trunk. Her eyes raked across his face, down his chest, and then she locked her gaze with his. Her chest rose and fell, her breathing coming in rapid bursts.

"Do I frighten you?" he whispered.

She shook her head, and his patience fled. Bending his head, he brushed her lips with his. A jolt shot through his body, desire flaring hotter than he'd ever known. He flattened against her, trailing kisses across her jaw, down her neck. He heard the gasp and smiled before claiming her mouth in a searing kiss. Her hands came around his collar, fingers scraping his scalp, signaling she was as hungry as he was.

Sam's blood pounded in his ears as his tongue traced the seam of her mouth. She opened for him, and he entered that heavenly space, tongues clashing, dueling, leaving them both breathless. When he ended the kiss, he kept his forehead against hers, breathing heavily. "I knew it would be like this." It had been better than his dreams. A blessing or a curse?

"I apologize for my... for..." His desire? His passion? But he wasn't sorry.

She shook her head. "Don't. We'll spoil it."

He nodded, and with a deep breath, he stepped away, tucking her arm in his once again as they made their way back to the path. Sam had a ridiculous smile on his face. He could feel it, and he didn't care. That kiss. That kiss had been—

"So, do you have plans for the future, Dr—Sampson?" she asked breathily.

He reluctantly came back to earth and scrambled to gather his thoughts. "I have an office for my practice, but as I gain experience, I'd like to mentor young doctors at one of the hospitals. Perhaps my own hospital. There are so many in need of care and so few good physicians. The medical field is changing, growing, and I want to be a part of it." Did he sound pompous or passionate? He hoped the latter. "And you?"

"America. I'm saving my money and starting a new life in America."

Sam's stomach plummeted to his knees.

CHAPTER 9

*W*hy had she blurted that out? After *such* a kiss? She'd panicked.

Never had a kiss affected her like that. As a married woman, the marital bed had been pleasant, her husband's attentions ardent, enthusiastic. But this... this was a brand-new, breathtaking experience.

She'd felt passion before, so what was this even more intense emotion?

Dottie wondered how her legs held her up as they walked back to the curricle. She was sure if she let go of Sampson's arm, she would crumple to the ground. When his lips touched hers, nothing had existed except his mouth on hers, his breath against her skin. It was frightening and deliriously wonderful.

Sampson helped her into the curricle and paid the boy. She heard him thank the lad for putting the top up, and the boy's gasp when given a coin. Climbing in, Sampson clucked to the horses, his beaver hat back in place, his face a polite mask to any passerby. No one would ever know they had just shared an earth-shattering moment. For Dottie was no longer sure what love was. Her limited experience had not prepared her for the touch of this man, the genuine goodness she saw him in.

"So tell me, why America?" His soft voice had a new pitch to it. Hurt, perhaps?

"Why not?" She shrugged. "I thought the farther away I went, the easier it would be to start again."

"Running from memories?"

The clack of the horses' hooves echoed in a taunting rhythm against the cobblestone.

Tell him. Tell him. Tell him.

But the words wouldn't come. Her feelings were too new, and she wasn't sure how she felt about… anything. Him, that kiss, leaving England. She was so confused. Would he tell people who she really was if she confided in him? Her instincts screamed no, but her instincts had been wrong before.

Sam bumped her shoulder with his, and there was a lighter tone to his words. "We can make new memories here, together."

Dottie blinked back tears. Why couldn't she have met him first? She was damaged goods now, and he deserved so much more. He pulled up on the reins, and she realized they were back at the tavern.

"Have I done something? Should I have waited longer to kiss you?" he asked, tipping her chin with a knuckle and turning her face toward him. "I think about you all the time. You are in my dreams when I close my eyes, in my thoughts as I drink my morning coffee or take my supper. And when we kissed, I knew you had found your way *here*." He took her hand and held it against his chest. Even through his great-coat, she could feel the steady *thump* of his heart.

"We hardly know one another," she managed weakly, her resolution failing.

He shook his head. "We've been meeting for over two months. Many couples marry after a courtship of that length."

She opened her mouth, but he put a finger against her lips.

"No, you aren't ready for a proposal, but I don't think it's too soon to tell you how I feel. I was not alone under that tree. It was a mutual passion." He leaned forward and brushed her lips, once, twice. "Can you deny there is something between us?"

Dottie shook her head. "There is so much you don't know about me." Her words were a ragged whisper. "And there's Violet. She's become my responsibility."

"We have nothing but time, Dottie. I don't know what you've been through. There is a haunted expression I see in your beautiful eyes when you think I'm not looking. I want to know everything about your past and Violet's." He kissed her forehead. "There are bits of mine you will learn, and I hope we will not judge each other."

"I have no right to judge anyone." She shook her head, laid her hand on his cheek. "You are a good, caring man. One who will make a difference in people's lives."

"Let us make a difference together. I have an idea for a hospital for unmarried mothers. You could be an important part of that. I need someone by my side with intelligence, a partner, who can help me with my plans. One who would understand the girls—women—and educate them to be independent, self-sufficient." His eyes were almost brown in the dim light, but his excitement shone brightly. "Who better to help those in need, than those who have walked their same path?"

With a deep breath, she nodded. There was a ring of truth to that statement. The downtrodden knew how disingenuous the upper class could be, doling out aid which always included stipulations. What Sampson offered was sincere—assistance on their terms, giving them ways to help themselves long after they left the hospital.

"Will you think about it?" he asked. His voice was husky as his thumb stroked her jaw, and she leaned her cheek into his palm.

Dottie closed her eyes when his lips touched hers. At that moment, she could deny him nothing. She would have to find the right time to tell him about Robert. And prayed he would understand.

* * *

THE NEXT DAY

Sampson rose from the dining room table to fetch the port. Mrs. Olssen had fixed a delicious meal of guinea hen, mashed turnips, carrots, fresh bread, and pear tarts for dessert. Her husband had broken his nose, no explanation requested or offered, and in return for setting the bone, she had provided a delicious dinner. Sam had bought the fowl, and Mrs. Olssen and her daughter had taken care of the rest.

"I have to say this bartering for services is delicious," said Benjamin. He wiped his mouth with a napkin and ran a hand through his dark-blond hair. "I haven't had custard that good in ages."

Clayton shook his head and patted his belly. "I agree. Thank you for the invitation. You could have had three more meals out of this if we hadn't helped."

"True, but I'd have missed the fascinating intellectual repartee of my brothers." Sam grinned as he returned with the port and poured three glasses. He looked at his two brothers, so different yet so much in common.

Ben was quieter, more studious, with a slighter frame and lighter coloring. Clayton was heavily muscled, though not barrel-chested like Harry, with darker coloring. There was nothing quiet and assuming about Clayton. He enjoyed socializing and had a natural confidence that Sam and Ben had always envied as children. Of course, Clay's self-assurance and adventurous spirit had also been the cause of *mis*adventures when they were younger, as Sam and Ben had always been eager to follow his lead.

"Remember the time we thought Old Man Wheeler was kidnapping babies?" asked Ben, shaking his head. The elderly eccentric had lived next door, always ranting about his "lazy Irish" neighbors, the beggars on the street corners harassing hardworking folk, and the upstart radicals wanting change. "Now I understand Paddy and Maggie took pity on the lonely widower and didn't want the neighborhood children taunting him. But they should have told us that instead of making Wheeler out to be a villain."

SAM TOOK the first step of the portico, then paused. What was that noise? He waited for it to come again—a high-pitched mewling. He ran up the rest of the steps and burst into the hallway. No one was in the parlor, and only Cook was in the kitchen.

"Have you seen Ben or Clay, ma'am?" he asked her, hopping from one foot to another.

She gave the dough on the table a final pat, wiped her floured hands on her apron, and turned to him with her hands on her hips. "What's got your fur flyin', Sampson?"

He only shook his head. "Just need to find them."

"Last I saw, they were following August out back."

He ran for the rear door.

"Fresh biscuits in the tin," Cook called after him.

He slid to a stop, backed up several steps, and opened the canister. The smell of molasses and oats tickled his nose. Grabbing four, he murmured a quick "thank you" and let the door slam behind him.

Sam saw Gus's large frame first. He was standing under a tree, a bucket of water in his hand, and Dublin the wolfhound tied to the tree trunk. Clayton clutched a piece of soap, and Ben held a brush and towel.

"What happened to Dublin?"

"He rolled in something dead, I figure," answered Gus. "Dead fish, I think. Maggie says he can't come back in the house until he's had a bath."

"Are those biscuits all for you?" asked Clayton, a smirk on his face as he held a hand out.

Sam shook his head. "Got one for all of us."

"Let me have mine before I'm wet as a rat in the Thames," Gus said, scratching the wolfhound's wiry gray coat.

They ate their biscuits, enjoying the shade beneath the leafy boughs. The sound of munching and a tail thumping the ground in hopeful participation punctuated the momentary silence.

Gus finished, wiping his mouth with his forearm and wiping his hands together to dust off the crumbs. "Sam, you can hold Dublin's collar while I douse him with water. Clayton will soap him up, we'll all scrub, then I'll rinse him."

They all nodded solemnly. Giving this giant beast a bath was no easy feat, and every one of them would end up as wet as the canine. Sam was surprised the dog only shook his coat twice while they were scrubbing. Ben laughed when Gus got suds in his eyes, but the smile quickly faded with a glare from the bigger boy.

By the time they had finished, Dublin was rolling in the grass, determined to find a bit of anything to rid himself of the clean scent. Cook had brought out lemonade, and the boys sat sprawled on any patch of fairly dry grass they could find.

"So why did you come running out here with that funny look on your face?" asked Ben.

Sam had almost forgotten. "I heard some odd noises coming from Old Man Wheeler's house."

"Don't go over there," warned Gus. "Maggie will take a switch to you."

The boys all snorted at the thought of the Irish woman laying a hand to any of them.

Gus pointed a beefy finger at Clayton. "Don't go getting no ideas, Clay. O'Briens said to stay away, and we will stay away. It ain't our business what noises come out of his house."

Clayton glared back. "Why are you only pointing at me? Sam's the one who brought it up."

Gus let out a loud, pained sigh. "Fine, I'll tell you the secret. But you got to swear not to let Paddy and Maggie know I told you."

All three boys leaned forward, eyes wide.

"He eats babes for breakfast. No one's ever been able to catch him, so the adults make sure us kids stay far away from him." Gus leaned back against the trunk of the tree, his arms crossed over his wide chest. "You can imagine what he'd do with bigger ones. Put 'em on a spit and roast 'em for supper."

"August," Cook called from the back door, "Mrs. O'Brien needs ye."

Gus stood, towering over the boys. Although Sam was older, he knew better than to cross Gus, especially when he seemed so serious. "Remember what I said and stay away from there."

LATER THAT NIGHT, sitting outside in the dusk, Sam heard the noise again, and his stomach clenched.

"Was that what you were talking about?" Ben whispered.

"It sounds like babies crying," Clayton said in a half whisper. "Do you think we should take a look?"

Ben shook his head. "You heard what Gus told us. We can't. It's too dangerous."

Clayton squinted at the dark form of the neighbor's house. "What if we went when Wheeler was gone?"

Sam brightened. "That's right. It would be safe as long as he was gone."

Ben wasn't convinced. "I don't think it's a good idea. If we get caught, Maggie really will take a switch to us."

"You've got as much courage as baby Nora." Clayton grinned. "You stay here and suck on your thumb. Me and Sam will go save the babes. We'll be heroes."

"You'll be dead heroes on a spit." Ben stuck his chin out.

"What if we don't do anything, and he gets Nora somehow?" asked Sam, his chest tightening at the thought.

Ben thought about it, his eyes growing wide. "How do we know if he's gone?"

"Simple. If there ain't no lights on in the house, he's gone," Clayton said matter-of-factly.

Clay fetched a candle, and the boys walked around the house but saw no lights. They snuck down the stairs to the cellar and tried the door. It was locked, but with a bit of jigging and a handy piece of wire, it was soon open.

Clay led the way as they followed the soft cries. Sam's heart pounded so loud that he was sure Gus would hear it next door. But what they found astonished them more than a dozen babes could have. In a box with a blanket was a small terrier with a litter of tiny pups. They squirmed against their mama's belly, eyes barely open.

"Puppies!" cried all three boys, crowding around the box and petting both the mother and her squirming babies.

"So this is where you disappeared to Sadie," said Clay. "I thought she'd run away because the old man was so mean."

"I want one," said Sam, tickling the ear of the runt. It was black and white, and it latched on to Sam's fingertip, sucking with gusto.

"Won't get nothin' out of there," Ben said with a laugh.

"What in the devil are you nodcocks doing here?" rasped a voice behind them.

They froze, and Sam closed his eyes, fear freezing his bones. He vaguely wondered what Maggie would do when none of them returned home.

"W-we thought you w-were..." Ben swallowed hard.

"Were what? Speak up, you dirty little curs." Old Man Wheeler raised his fist, waving his walking stick at them.

"We thought we heard babies down here," said Clayton, his voice tremulous.

"Why would I have squealing infants here when I don't even have a wife?" griped the old man.

"Because you eat them for breakfast!" cried Sam.

"You'll never get our sister. Never!" added Ben. "RUN!"

Clayton took the lead again. As he put out a hand to push the old man out of their path, Wheeler stepped back, placing his cane on each backside as they passed. The boys howled up the steps and ran for the safety of home.

"You had nerves of steel even as a boy," Sam said to Clayton. "I thought we'd be roasted and our bones tossed in the alley."

"The look on the old goat's face when he found us playing with the pups." Ben pretended a shiver. "My legal mind shudders at the thought of the laws we broke. Breaking and entering, theft—"

"I really wanted that little black and white puppy," Sam remembered, his shoulders shaking. "Instead, we received a scolding and no supper that night."

"I thought we were going to get away with it until Dublin started howling when we came running from the cellar. Of course, Paddy was just coming home." Clayton shook his head. "He was soooo angry with us."

They sat in silence for a bit, each remembering their own version of the childhood tale.

"There's been a development in the Ferguson case," Clayton said, ending the quiet.

"The man found in the Thames?" asked Ben. "A shame that happened when he'd tried to escape his criminal past."

"Sometimes regret comes too late," Sam agreed. "What's come up?"

Clayton let out a long sigh. "It seems Mr. and Mrs. Ferguson also had a young daughter. The landlady is worried for her and wanted us to see if we could find her."

"That shouldn't be too hard. A young girl, one of hundreds, wandering the streets. I'm sure you'll find her by morning," quipped Ben.

"Ha-ha! I asked Roger to ask around about the girl. He has plenty of connections and comes from the rookery." Roger Lynch was a newcomer to the O'Brien clan. Walters had intervened when the lad had been attacked in an alley. Paddy had hired the boy to do odd jobs, chauffeur the ladies, and whatever else might be needed at any given time. Just sixteen, Roger had a strong fist and was trying to work his way up to a Peeler.

"How's he working out? I put over a dozen stitches in that arm when Harry found him that night," said Sam.

"We keep him busy, especially Maggie. And Paddy is thrilled because he doesn't have to go shopping anymore. I see potential in him." Clayton got up and poured himself more port and held up the decanter to his brothers. Both nodded and he refilled their glasses. "I wonder about the mother's death. It's not that unusual for a robbery to go wrong and the victim end up dead. Especially if they put up a fight. But it's the timing. I had Eli take a look at the report."

Eli was the only Peeler still working for Bow Street. He

had easy—and legal, as Ben always emphasized—access to the reports filed.

"Seems she was murdered just after Ferguson quit working for The Vicar. Like I said, it's not how she died but when she died. A warning? A punishment?" Clayton shook his head. "I pray that little girl is somewhere safe."

CHAPTER 10

Sunday
St. James's Park

"*H*urry, sweeting, or we won't get a prime spot."
It was another warm day for November, so she'd decided to take Violet with her. It would be good for the girl to get some fresh air. And meet Dr. Brooks.

Dottie had made a decision. She would find the words to explain how she'd become a widow, then let fate decide if she should stay or go to America. Her heart told her that Sampson meant what he said about a future together. If he would have her, she would be a part of his life, his plans.

Besides, the voyage had lost its appeal. The Clatterlys had helped her establish a living. She was able to support herself, and soon, she wouldn't need a reference. Her landlords and their patrons already sang her praises. Violet had settled in and seemed happy with their lot.

"I don't mind if you walk around and enjoy the day but don't wander too far. I want to properly introduce you to Samps—Dr. Brooks. He may become someone important to me, so the two of you need to become acquainted." Dottie ignored the pouty look and patted the girl's cheek. "You look very pretty in your new gown. The deep green makes your hair look golden."

Violet grinned and ran off toward the canal. "Don't muss your clothes and keep your pelisse on. It's not *that* warm!" Dottie called after her.

By the time Sampson arrived, her nerves had calmed. "Good day, fine sir. May I interest you in a treat? I'm told I make the very best tarts in London."

"Funny thing. I was told the same." He leaned over her cart, squinting at the pastries. "They don't look so extraordinary to me."

She gasped in mock offense, then grinned when he winked at her. "I'm glad you've come."

"Are you? I wasn't quite sure how we'd left things on Wednesday." Relief shone on his face. "Shall we continue our Wednesdays, then?"

She nodded. "However, there are some things about my past I must share with you before—"

"Before I lose my heart? Too late, Dottie." He took off his hat and ran a hand through his brown waves. "There is one burning question on my mind that isn't related to my heart. Well, it is but not romantically."

"Yes?" What in the world could he want to know that had to do with his heart but not lo—romance?

"I've mentioned my desire to open a hospital and school for women who find themselves with child and alone."

He hesitated, his face growing red, and she wondered if she'd somehow embarrassed him.

"I believe I've found a suitable building, and I thought…

well, I thought you might go with me to look at it?" His hazel eyes studied the ground after the question.

She thought he was adorable, like a boy who'd asked to kiss the girl and waited for her answer. "I'd be delighted. But I'm not very knowledgeable about the running of a hospital."

"The building will also provide housing for the girls, and they will be schooled there. As a very qualified instructor, your opinion would mean a great deal to me." He glanced up at her, probably gauging her reaction.

A smile spread across her face. "I would love to volunteer once it is set up. Do you have a name yet?" She had missed teaching. The satisfaction of shaping the life of someone for the better did something for her soul. It filled a void inside her that she hadn't realized was there until she'd married. Dottie appreciated her pastry work, but it wasn't the same as teaching. Watching the light in a child's eyes when they learn to read or a young woman's delight at realizing she can learn as well as any man. If only…

"I hope you consider being in charge of the school, taking care of the day-to-day running of it, hiring more instructors, deciding the curriculum. All subjects *I* know little about." His gaze locked with hers now. "We could make quite a team."

Dottie's breath caught as she saw a future with Sampson spread before her, helping others, helping each other. Then she remembered her news. "I brought Violet along today. It's time the two of you meet." Dottie needed time to think about the doctor's proposition. It was so very tempting and much more suited to her than being a costermonger.

"The magical child who tames the beastly barkeep?"

Dottie chuckled and scanned the expanse of lawn on either side of them. "One and the same."

"Is she hiding in the cart?" he asked with a straight face, poking at the cakes and pasties.

"She disappears each time I have a customer, then gets

bored, I suppose, and returns. The last time I saw her, she was following a couple toward the canal."

"Is that her?"

Dottie saw Violet approaching them at a run. "Yes, and she managed to stay clean. Miracles on a Sunday."

The girl stopped just behind Dottie, clinging to her pelisse and peeking around at Sampson. In the distance a constable's whistle blew, and the sound of pedestrians laughing floated on the slight breeze.

"Violet, this is Dr. Brooks."

"Miss Violet, it's a pleasure to finally meet you."

Violet stared at him solemnly, and Dottie wondered what was going on in that little brain of hers.

"And yes, I *am* enjoying this fine November day. Thank you for inquiring," Sampson said with a grin, his dimples deepening as he tried to charm Violet. His questioning eyes looked to Dottie.

"I'm afraid she doesn't speak. I've heard her laugh or hum along when I sing but never words." Her arm went around the slim frame protectively. "I understand she's capable, but something must have happened…"

"Fascinating—and tragic, of course." He cocked his head, studying Violet. "I've heard of the phenomena with soldiers in battle. A traumatic incident that keeps them from speaking, some blocked memory too painful to remember."

"Is there a cure?" Dottie realized she should have shared this information sooner. Sampson might be able to treat Violet.

"Time, usually." He squatted down to Violet's level. "You're a lucky girl to have found Mrs. Brown."

Violet nodded and clutched Dottie's skirt more tightly.

Sampson stood and tousled the girl's hair. "I'd like a dozen of everything you've brought."

She chuckled and decided not to argue this time. When

she handed him the package, he reached inside his greatcoat and pulled out his purse, dropping some coins into her hand. "Until Wednesday, Mrs. Brown."

He tipped his hat and walked away, whistling some jaunty tune.

Violet stepped to the front of the cart and watched him leave. A small group approached from the opposite direction, catching Dottie's attention while they considered what to buy, and when she looked around, the girl was gone again.

A few minutes later, another whistle blew, closer this time. A man's shout, then a terrifying scream that sent a chill down Dottie's back.

Dottie picked up her skirts and ran toward the commotion. Somehow, she knew it was Violet. Had she fallen into the canal? In the distance, she saw Sampson carrying the child, kicking and screaming. As he drew closer, a constable close behind, she could see Violet's tear-streaked face.

"Maaaamaaaa!"

The breath left Dottie's lungs. Sampson struggled to hold on to the girl, who was striking out at some invisible obstacle, fingers clawing at the air, her brown eyes glazed and unseeing.

Sampson stopped at the cart, leaning against a tree as he lowered himself and the hysterical girl to the ground. Dottie was on her knees in an instant, stroking her hair, murmuring soothing words. Violet's flailing subsided. She leaned against Dottie's chest, whimpering and clutching at her shoulders.

The constable stood over them, a stern look on his face. "What's going on here?"

Sampson gently laid the child in Dottie's lap and stood. "My name is Dr. Brooks. I'm afraid this child has had some kind of fit. I believe it's over for now."

The man's bushy eyebrows came together as he stared at

Dottie and the trembling girl. "Well, I s'pose you would know more about it than me. Do you need any help with the lass?"

"No, but I thank you."

"Been a busy day. Four pockets picked today and now this." The constable nodded. "Well, if you don't need my help, I'll be off. Good luck with the little one. Poor thing."

Dottie rocked Violet, holding her close and trying not to cry. "What happened?"

"We'll discuss it later. She may have remembered something." He squatted down and brushed wet hair from the girl's face. "I'll get a hackney to take you both home, then find someone to bring your cart to the Clatterlys. Perhaps the boy who is holding Jack."

Dottie nodded, so thankful that Sampson had been there. "Will you come and check on her?"

"Of course. Once she's home, get her into bed and use a cool compress to ease the pain in her head. I'd imagine she has a megrim after all this." He straightened. "Don't worry, she'll be fine."

CHAPTER 11

Sam wondered how he would tell Dottie what the girl had done. At the time, his main concern had been for the health of the child. She was a little thief and had probably been at it all afternoon. He imagined she'd been taught how to pick pockets from the time she could walk. But why today? Habit? After arranging for Dottie's cart to be returned, he'd stopped by his office for his satchel and a tincture in case Violet was restless.

He knocked on the back door of the tavern, and Mrs. Clatterly answered it, spying his bag. "Oh, Dr. Brooks. You're a saint. The poor little mite is asleep now, but Mrs. Brown is…" The landlady sighed and showed him to the room, leaving the door open as she backed away. "I'll get you some tea."

Dottie sat at a wooden table, staring at four small purses in front of her. When he entered, she looked up at him, her eyes brimming with tears.

It seemed his explanation might not be as lengthy as he'd thought. "You found them in her pelisse?" He removed his greatcoat and hung it on a hook next to the door. Setting his satchel on the table, he took out the tincture and handed it to her.

"If she becomes restless during the night, give her two drops of this, no more. It will make her drowsy, so she can relax and go back to sleep."

She nodded, then pointed to the stolen pouches. "Why?"

"I was wondering the same thing." He sank into a chair next to her and took her hand. "When I caught her reaching into my greatcoat and snatched her up, she went berserk. I thought bringing her to you might calm her. And it did, eventually."

"She s-stole from you?" Her voice cracked with pain. "I'm so sorry."

"Why don't we start at the beginning. Tell me how the two of you met."

At this, the tears streamed down her face, a sob escaping. "I was going to tell you on Wednesday, explain everything."

Apprehension skittered down his spine. "Explain what?"

"We met at a hanging." She gazed at him with pleading eyes.

"The same day I first saw you?" he asked, releasing her hand. "We've never discussed that."

Dottie closed her eyes and nodded.

"In hindsight, I realize she was being chased. But I asked her if she was there with someone, and she pointed to the gallows." She swallowed and opened her eyes. "Her brother was the young man standing next to Robert."

He blinked. "Robert Dunn?" His heart pounded as he waited for a trap door to open beneath *him*. "And how would you know Robert Dunn?"

"He was my husband. Brown is my family name."

Sam shook his head in disbelief. He needed to breathe. He needed time to examine this new revelation. "You couldn't have been married to that man. He was… he was—"

"A murderer. Yes, I know." She reached for his hand, and he pulled it back. "I had no idea who he was. I thought he worked for a vicar of a wealthy parish."

"The Vicar, a criminal with no conscience who we've been after for months. How could you not know?" He was shouting now and stood, sucking in a deep breath to calm himself.

"I was naïve and believed his façade of a gentleman. There was no one to guide me except a spinster who ran a girls' school. She was fooled as well. I didn't know until the constable knocked on our door and arrested him."

"*Your husband* worked for the man who was responsible for my mother's death and my family's ruin." He ran his hand through his hair, pacing the room. "He sold the insurance certificate to my father. When I was finally able to pay off the debt, it was too late. My mother's health was so poor, she only lived another six months. My father died within the year. Most likely of a broken heart."

"Why were you at Newgate that day?" she asked, her voice growing cold.

"To watch The Vicar's men hang."

"And the man responsible for their arrest?"

"Paddy O'Brien."

They stared at one another, at an impossible impasse.

Mr. Clatterly burst into the room, Mrs. Clatterly right behind him with a tea tray. He took one look at the Dottie, then at Sam. "I think you should leave now."

* * *

ONCE HER LANDLORDS were assured she was fine, Mr. Clatterly led her into the closed public room. "I think you need a strong tonic, so you'll sleep." His voice was gruff, but affection warmed his tone. He handed her a small glass of brandy, then poured one for his wife and himself.

"I can't believe the good doctor was so upset over a pickpocket. He didn't lose anything," sniffed Mrs. Clatterly. "I thought he was better than that."

"He is," agreed Dottie. "I'm afraid there's much more to our story than that."

Mr. Clatterly pulled out a chair for her, and they all sat at the table close to the hearth. The dying embers popped and glowed, and Dottie just wanted to lose her thoughts in the bright orange and yellows. Between the brandy and the hot coals, the chill in her bones was subsiding. She inhaled deeply and began her tale.

"I am so sorry to have deceived you, but I didn't know what else to do. I had to survive," Dottie ended lamely, afraid to look her landlords in the eye. "You have become dear friends, and I would do anything to start again."

Mr. Clatterly sat with his lips pursed, arms crossed over his chest. He grunted. Mrs. Clatterly rose and threw her arms around Dottie in a tight hug.

"You poor, poor dear. What you've been through and how you must have suffered." The older woman wiped at her eyes with the hem of her apron. "Of course we forgive you, don't we, Husband?"

He looked up with a brusque nod. "I'd have happily strangled the rat myself if given the chance. Takin' advantage of a young innocent like that."

The relief swept over Dottie like an ocean wave, and tears spilled down her cheeks. "Thank you so much, both of you, for… everything. Taking me in, befriending me, welcoming Violet. You are the best of people!"

"Nonsense," argued Mrs. Clatterly, "we've done nothin' any other decent human being wouldn't do. Now dry your eyes and finish your brandy. Dr. Brooks will see his way back to you."

"And if he don't, he don't deserve the likes of a fine woman as yourself," added Mr. Clatterly, awkwardly patting her shoulder. "He'll keep a civil tone if he comes under my roof again."

After the couple returned to their apartment above the tavern, Dottie remained in the public room, considering the afternoon and all that had transpired. Sam's father had been the one to ensure Robert's arrest, beginning her own downward spiral. Yet, she couldn't blame him for apprehending a criminal. Her husband had been a terrible man. So her initial anger toward Sampson had evaporated.

Instead, she looked inward and tried to see how the news must have affected him. Robert had been one of the men responsible for the ruin of not only his family, but a young boy's life and future. The terror he must have felt as a boy when the foundation beneath him crumbled away. How could she fix this? An apology seemed so feeble. And she certainly hadn't meant to deceive him.

And then there was Violet. Why had the girl resorted to pickpocketing? She had clothes, food, shelter, and love. Dottie knew in her heart that the girl wasn't a bad seed. So what had caused her to—

She closed her eyes, remembering Violet's cries and gestures. Dottie saw the girl putting her hands together and making the symbol for a boat on the water. Oh, no! A hand went to her mouth as the little girl's motive hit her like a brick to the forehead.

She was stealing money for tickets to America. They counted their funds frequently, and Violet had been upset when Dr. Brooks had entered their world. Did she think, if Dottie and Sam were to marry, she would be cast aside?

Dottie rose and returned to her own room. She added

more coal to the stove, then undressed and climbed into bed with Violet. The girl had not stirred. Dottie wrapped her arms around her, holding her close, going over the conversation they would have in the morning. She had put away the stolen pouches, wondering how they might be returned.

She didn't have the strength tonight to think about it. Tomorrow.

Tomorrow would be soon enough.

Tonight, her heart was broken.

CHAPTER 12

*S*ampson spent a sleepless night filled with nightmares. He was chasing Dottie, but each time he caught her, he saw Robert Dunn's face. Then his mother's. He needed a voice of reason and knew where to go.

Margaret answered the door herself. "Why, 'tis our Sam. Paddy," she called over her shoulder, "Sam's come."

He followed her into the dining room, where the redheaded giant was filling his plate from the sideboard. "Grab a plate, boyo."

Sam shook his head. "I'm not hungry. I came for advice."

Paddy's blue eyes narrowed. "Ye look like death. What happened?"

After pouring a cup of coffee, he sank into a chair. "It's a long story."

Margaret kissed him on the cheek. "We've nowhere to go. Tell us your tale."

Sampson told them the whole sordid story. When he finished, his coffee was cold.

"So, she ain't Mrs. Brown?" asked Paddy.

"No, she was Miss Dorothea Brown before she married."

He gulped down the cold black liquid and stood to pour himself another. "And Clayton might be interested in the girl."

"Easy enough to find out if her brother swung next to Dunn." Paddy smeared some jam on his bread and said around a mouthful, "We'll let Clay know. He'll have sumtin' before da end of da week."

"What about Dottie?" Both men turned to look at Margaret. "I can't imagine what she's going t'rough."

"What *she's* going through? She lied to me—about her name, who she was." Sam stood abruptly, almost sending his chair crashing to the floor. He began to pace. "All this time I thought she was a widow—"

"She *is* a widow," Margaret said quietly, "who was duped by a man. Just like those women ye help at Magdalen. Only she didn't end up at a hospital, begging for help. She made her own way da best she could."

Sam opened his mouth, then closed it, letting Margaret's words sink in.

"I doubt she could get any *decent* work using da name Dunn. So, she took back Brown and found a way to survive. A way other than prostitution. Tell me, Sampson J. Brooks, what ye would've done in her position." Margaret's chin stuck out as she held his gaze. "In my humble opinion, she's a brave young woman, and yer lucky to know her."

Paddy whistled. "Well, ain't it just like my lovely wife to cut right to da thick of it."

"That's why she wanted to start over in America." Sam hung his head. "No one would know her."

"I imagine she couldn't find a position without a reference. Da poor dear," Margaret said. "And my Sam shouts at her. Shame on ye."

"But—"

"Ye love her, boyo?" asked Paddy.

"What does that have to do with anything?"

"Answer him, Sam."

With a snort, he nodded.

"'Tis settled then."

"It's not that simple."

Margaret snorted this time. "Aye, it is. Yer mother followed yer father into King's Bench out of love. Ye took to da streets out of love. Yer woman told a lie, 'tis all. How can love not conquer dat?"

Sam stared at the wise woman before him. Yes indeed. If he could bottle her insight, they'd all be as rich as Croesus.

* * *

FRIDAY

VIOLET HAD NOT SPOKEN AGAIN. She had been terrified Dottie would send her away. She'd been right; Violet thought Dottie would marry Dr. Brooks, leaving her alone. She had stolen the money, hoping to leave for America before that happened.

The rest of the week was a blur. She had no idea what to do with the stolen purses, so she'd given them to the Clatterlys. They had passed them on to a constable, saying a fleeing pickpocket had dropped them outside the tavern.

"You can't mope around forever, my dear," said Mrs. Clatterly as she helped Dottie load her cart. "Will you try to speak with Dr. Brooks?"

She shook her head. Her landlady had been much more understanding when told about Dottie's past than Sampson had been. Not that she could blame him. It had all come to light in the worst possible way. And it was devastating to know he was somehow connected to the worst time in her life.

"He was surprised and hurt. Who wouldn't be?" Mrs. Clatterly smiled at Violet. "But look how he worried over our little girl, even knowing what she'd done. He's still a good man, I say."

That was the hardest part. Sampson *was* a good man. If only she could turn back time.

"Violet!" called Mr. Clatterly from the public room. "Violet!"

The girl wiped her hands on her apron and ran out of the room. A few minutes later, she returned with a grin on her face. She took Dottie's hand and began pulling her toward the tavern.

"I don't have time, sweeting. It's time for me to leave."

Violet shook her head and pulled harder. Mrs. Clatterly went to the doorway and peeked out. "Saints and sinners!" she said. "Dottie, you're needed in the front."

Irritated, she took off her redingote and walked into the tavern. "Mr. Clatterly—"

He pointed at the entrance.

Sampson stood there, his greatcoat dusted with snow, a lopsided smile on his face. He cleared his throat. "I was wondering if I might have a word with you?"

"Why?" Her heart couldn't take one more crumb of disappointment.

"I-I have information concerning Violet." His hazel eyes pinned hers, daring her to say no.

"About Sunday?"

"About her family."

All the fight went out of her. She nodded and moved to a table next to the kitchen. There were only a few customers at the moment, and they were seated at the other end of the room.

Sampson took a chair next to her. "The Clatterlys are welcome to hear this if you'd like."

"Yes, I would." They would give her strength.

Mrs. Clatterly made tea, and they all sat at the table, listening to Sampson's tale.

"So, her name is Violet Ferguson?" asked Mrs. Clatterly again. "There's no way she could have told us that with hand motions."

"No," agreed Sampson. "The father and son both worked for Robert Dunn. Before that, they were pickpockets and taught Violet the trade. That, however, has nothing to do with why she doesn't speak.

"She and her mother were set upon one night by two men. Her mother put up a fight, and according to a witness, Violet tried to kick and bite the attackers. One of them caught her, holding her back as the other pushed her mother and grabbed her bag. She fell and hit her head. The men fled, leaving Violet crying over her mother's lifeless body."

He paused, letting them think about the news. "According to the landlady, she hasn't spoken since then."

"Oh, my heavens." Mrs. Clatterly shook her head and dabbed her eyes with her apron.

Mr. Clatterly scowled.

Dottie reached for Sampson's hand without thought. How her chest hurt, but now it was for Violet. When he squeezed her fingers in return, then reached across the table, and wiped a tear from her cheek, the river flowed. He pulled a handkerchief from his waistcoat and handed it to her.

"Will she ever speak again?" she asked.

Sampson shrugged. "I don't know. It's possible. But I believe when I grabbed her last Sunday, that memory—or parts of it—came flooding back."

"Thank you for coming to tell us." Dottie blew her nose,

then chewed her bottom lip, wondering if she should give the handkerchief back.

"I'm sorry for Violet. And I'm sorry for losing my temper."

"No, you have nothing to apologize for," she said. "I—"

"Had to survive, as my second mother pointed out." He put his other hand over hers. "I will say this in front of the Clatterlys. In front of all London if I must. I love you, Dottie Brown or Dunn or whatever name you decide to take. You have an inner strength to match my own, and I can't imagine a better woman by my side."

She sniffed and blew her nose again. Definitely not giving it back until she washed it. *I can't imagine a better woman by my side.* Her gaze snapped to his face. That crooked smile again.

"Paddy always says a person should try to follow bad news with good news. I hope you consider this good news." He cleared his throat. "Dottie, would you be my wife, my partner in life?"

She swallowed. This week had been miserable, thinking she'd never see him again. "What about Violet?"

"Of course, she'd be welcome—"

"She's staying with us."

Three pairs of eyes turned to look at Mr. Clatterly. "You can spend all the time with her that you want, but we've an extra room upstairs. The lass considers this her home now. Ain't no one gonna upset her again."

"Could we leave it up to Violet?" asked Dottie, though she knew the little girl loved the couple dearly. She had never heard the man put so many words together at one time.

"She'll be our only daughter, never having to share with half siblings. We'd bring her up right." Mr. Clatterly had crossed his arms obstinately again, but this time his stubbornness was directed at his wife.

"I'm happy with whatever Violet decides," Mrs. Clatterly said and rose to kiss her husband on the cheek.

Dottie turned to Sampson. "Are you sure… *I* am what *you* want?"

"Never been more certain of anything."

"Then, yes."

"Heaven help us!" cried Mrs. Clatterly. "There's going to be a wedding!"

THE VICAR

Another part of London

He slammed his fist on the desk and glared at the men in front of him. He was alone now, allowing the anger to seep from him. Picking up the crystal tumbler, he threw back the last of the French brandy and hurtled the glass across the room.

The idiot Ferguson had been identified, and Bow Street magistrate was investigating. Dunn was gone, and he had to find someone competent to take his place. It was an inconvenience, not a huge setback, but it goaded him. He'd heard the rumors about the man's wife, blaming The Vicar. He ground his teeth. Wasn't he always generous with the widows? He would have set the woman up with a tidy pension, not murder her. As he'd tried for Dunn's widow, but she'd disappeared. There were limits to his violence. He drew the line at harming women and children. He wasn't a brute, an unfeeling beast who swept everything from his path without thought.

He was thoughtful, calculating, precise in his decisions.

Each plan drew him one step closer to his goal. Revenge would be his, no matter the years it took. So what if he became as wealthy as those titled devils in the process?

Bow Street was becoming a thorn in his side.

They were sniffing around one of his counterfeit businesses. He had interests everywhere, and it wouldn't break him to shut down and find a new location. But the men who'd been followed would have to be disposed of. This time there would be no bodies found. More importantly, he needed to find out who had so easily infiltrated his operations. He couldn't afford to have anything go wrong with his upcoming scheme.

EPILOGUE

Christmas Eve 1821

ottie carried the plum pudding to the dining room and set it in the center of the table. Mr. and Mrs. Clatterly sat across from her and Violet, with Sampson at the head of the table.

"Sam, would you light the plum pudding?" she asked him.

His heart was full. He had a beautiful wife, a babe on the way, a thriving practice, and his dream of a hospital for unmarried mothers was coming to fruition. He was truly blessed. He only wished his parents were here to see the "family" he had surrounding him.

Sam smiled as Dottie poured the brandy around the pudding. He went to the mantel and retrieved the tinder box. After lighting the stick, he handed it to Violet.

"I believe Violet should do the honors this year."

The lass had come so far. When given the choice, Violet had chosen to stay with the couple above the public house but remained a daily presence in Dottie and Sam's life. She was thriving with the Clatterlys, spent afternoons with Dottie for her lessons, and even spoke occasionally.

It had taken a few months, but the girl had finally warmed up to Sam. He had tried all his usual tricks—a multitude of smiles with his deepest dimples, trips to St. James's and Farrance's—and nothing had worked. Until he'd introduced her to the O'Briens and Aonarach. Violet had fallen in love with the giant hound and decided Sam was trustworthy after that. The bedraggled little waif would grow into a lovely young woman. And the Clatterlys beamed whenever they looked upon their daughter. Sampson knew how rare happy endings were outside of fairy tales. And he couldn't take credit for this one. It was all due to his beautiful, intelligent, caring wife.

Violet grinned and jumped from her chair, stopping to give Sam a kiss on his cheek. Carefully, she took the burning stick from his hand and held it to the pudding. They all clapped as the flame caught and lit up the dessert. Dottie and Mrs. Clatterly blinked back tears. Mr. Clatterly rubbed at his eyes.

"Happy Christmas," she whispered, and they all cheered.

REVIEWS ARE the lifeblood of authors. If you've enjoyed this story, please consider leaving a few words at your favorite retailer.

KEEP UPDATED ON FUTURE RELEASES, exclusive excerpts, and prizes by following my newsletter:
https://www.subscribepage.com/k3f1z5

AUTHOR'S NOTE

As my readers know, I always try to mix my stories with authentic places and real historical events. Here are some of the fun facts from this book:

Aonarach, the Irish wolfhound

The Irish wolfhound in this series is based on my own wolfhound, Solo. He was the only pup of his litter to survive. He overcame several major health issues, including gangrene in his tail that was docked. We received this big galoot at six months because he was pet quality and not eligible for the show ring. We didn't care. The name Aonarach (Ay-nuh-rok) means "only" in Irish Gaelic.

Magdalen House

Magdalen House was a hospital and home established in 1758 to take in "penitent prostitutes and young women" who had been seduced or shunned. Originally operating on the site of the old London Hospital in Prescott Street,

Whitechapel, a new building was built in July 1769 in St. George's Fields, Southwark. It was situated on the east side of the road leading from Blackfriars Bridge to the obelisk in St. George's Fields. Later, the hospital moved to Streatham and became a school in the 1930s.

New residents were admitted on the first Thursday of every month. Applicants visited the Magdalen and received a numbered, printed form from the clerk at the door. The women were called by number and interviewed by the board. They were judged on the sincerity and truth of their statements, and whether they truly wanted to reform or just hoped for a reprise from poverty. If a friend or relation accompanied the applicant, they were questioned separately to see if their testimony corroborated that of the woman.

Often there were at least twenty to thirty young women each month, mostly aged between sixteen and twenty-five, though sometimes younger. The committee had to choose the most deserving cases to fill the available spaces.

The Picture of London for 1810 stated the majority of those discharged were less than twenty years old. Pregnant applicants were turned away, along with those who had a venereal disease, usually treated at the Lock Hospital. The committee still tried to assist those who were not accepted by interceding on their behalf to family or friends or supporting them in some way until a spot became vacant.

What was life like in Magdalen House? The women underwent a probationary period, then separated into classes, according to their situation. There was an assistant to oversee each class, and a matron who ran the entire ward. It was called a hospital because its purpose was considered therapeutic. But the daily routine resembled a nunnery. According to the *Microcosm of London,*

This separation (useful on many accounts) is peculiarly so to a numerous class of women, who are much to be pitied, and to whom this charity has been very beneficial, viz young women who have been seduced from their friends under promises of marriage, and have been deserted by their seducers: they have never been in public prostitution, but fly to the Magdalen to avoid it: their relations, in the first moments of resentment, refuse to receive, protect, or acknowledge them; they are abandoned by the world, without character, without friends, without money, without resource, and wretched indeed is their situation!

To such especially, this house of refuge opens wide its doors; and instead of being driven by despair to lay violent hands on themselves, and to superadd the crime of self-murder to that guilt which is the cause of their distress, or of being forced, by the strong calls of hunger, into prostitution, they find a safe and quiet retreat in this abode of peace and reflection. To rescue from the threatening horrors of prostitution such victims of the base and ungenerous, whose ruin has frequently been more owing to their unsuspecting innocence, than to any other cause; to restore them to virtue and industry, after one false step, and to reconcile their friends, are considerations of the greatest magnitude.

The committee generally give such young women the preference, because they are almost certain of the best consequences; for it scarcely ever happens but their relations relent, when, by taking shelter in this house, they have given so strong a proof of their determination to quit a vicious way of life.

The women worked making linen or beadwork and earned a weekly wage. They were not encouraged to confide in others or make friends. Each ward posted a sign: *Tell your story to no one.*

The charity relied on benefactors who were often invited

and encouraged to visit the grounds. When potential donors were invited to the chapel for services, it became so popular that tickets were issued to keep the crowds down. Eventually, a collection taken at the door replaced the need for the tickets and provided a nicely sized donation to Magdalen House.

The first chaplain, William Dodd, said in one of his sermons, looking at the residents who stood behind a lattice but were still visible:

Lost to Virtue, you were lost to yourselves....Whither could you have fled from anguish, and from woe unutterable, cut off in the very blossom of your sins? early sacrifices, young and unpitied offerings to the remorseless Grave?.... 'Tis too affecting the review: I urge no more: only let your conversation be as becometh this great redemption: only labour to shew yourselves sensible of the exquisite blessings vouchsafed you....Here, saved from the threatening storm, you may look back and contemplate your danger, the more to inspire you with gratitude and praise.

As the Peelers' series continues, Dr. and Mrs. Brooks will establish the Hospital of Hope. I hope you enjoy their progress and enjoy meeting the occasional female in distress.

ABOUT THE AUTHOR

USA Today Bestselling author Aubrey Wynne resides in the Midwest with her husband, dogs, horses, mule, and barn cats. Obsessions include wine, history, travel, trail riding, and all things Christmas. Her Chicago Christmas series and historical romances have received multiple awards and nominations as a Rone finalist by InD'tale Magazine.

Aubrey's first love is medieval romance but after dipping her toe in the Regency period in 2018 with the *Wicked Earls' Club*, she was smitten. This inspired her sweet Regency spin-off series *Once Upon a Widow*, and a steamy Scottish Regency series, *A MacNaughton Castle Romance*. Her Regency detective series, *Paddy's Peelers*, will launch in 2025.

Social Media Links:
Website:
http://www.aubreywynne.com
Facebook:
https://www.facebook.com/magnificentvalor
Aubrey's Ever After Facebook group:
https://www.facebook.com/groups/
AubreyWynnesEverAfters/
Twitter:
https://twitter.com/Aubreywynne51
Pinterest:
https://www.pinterest.com/aubreywynne51/

Instagram:
https://www.instagram.com/Aubreywynne51
Bookbub page:
https://www.bookbub.com/profile/aubrey-wynne
Goodreads:
https://www.goodreads.com/author/show/7383937.
Aubrey_Wynne

Sign up for my newsletter and don't miss future releases
https://www.subscribepage.com/k3f1z5

ALSO BY AUBREY WYNNE

Once Upon a Widow series

Earl of Sunderland #1

Maggie award, International Digital Awards finalist

Christopher Roker inherited the title of rake. She hides behind her independence. Fate accepts the challenge…

Escaping his late brother's memory, Lady Grace is a welcome distraction. But as the attraction grows, Kit finds himself wavering between his old military life and the lure of an exceptional but unwilling woman.

A Wicked Earl's Widow #2

Recommended by InD'tale Magazine

Eliza, Lady Sunderland, is widowed after one year. Her abusive father, near financial ruin, is already planning another wedding.

When Viscount Pendleton discovers a beauty defending an elderly woman against ruffians, he is smitten. But Nate soon realizes he must discover Eliza's dark past to save the woman he loves.

Rhapsody and Rebellion #3

Maggie finalist, nominated for Rone Award, InD'tale Magazine

A Scottish legacy… A political rebellion… Two hearts destined to meet…

Alisabeth was betrothed from the cradle. At seventeen, she marries her best friend and finds happiness if not passion. In less than a year, a political rebellion makes her a widow. The handsome English earl arrives a month later and rouses her desire and a terrible guilt.

Crossing the border into Scotland, Gideon finds his predictable world turned upside down. Folklore, legend, and political unrest intertwine with an unexpected attraction to a feisty Highland beauty. When the earl learns of an English plot to stir the Scots into rebellion, he must choose his country or save the clan and the woman who stirs his soul.

Earl of Darby #4

Holt Medallion Winner, NTRWA Reader's Choice Award, Nominated for Rone Award, InD'tale magazine

Miss Hannah Pendleton, nursing her pride after her childhood crush falls in love with another, hurls herself into the excitement of a first season.

Since his wife's suicide on their wedding night, the Earl of Darby has carefully cultivated his rakish reputation. But when Nicholas sees a lovely newcomer being courted by the devil himself, her innocence and candor revive the chivalry buried deep in his soul.

Earl of Brecken #5

He's on the brink of ruin. She's in search of a hero.

Notorious for his seductive charm, the Earl of Brecken searches for a wealthy heiress. His choices are dismal until he meets Miss Franklin. Guileless, gorgeous and with an enormous dowry, she seems the answer to his prayers. Until his conscience makes an unexpected appearance.

Earl of Griffith #6

Sorrow and Regrets...

After eloping, a widowed Lady Helen is disillusioned with love and raising a three-year-old alone. Now she must face the music and her family.

An unexpected ray of sunshine...

Conway, Earl of Griffith is smitten at first sight with his friend's sister and adorable daughter. But can he convince the grieving and lovely widow that love is worth a second chance?

Beware A Wallflower's Wrath #7

Annis Craigg gave her heart—and innocence—away at seventeen. When Lord Robert Harding returns to Scotland fifteen years later, he's desperate to find the only woman he's ever loved. But she has secrets and an attitude.

Lies, secrets, and betrayal will challenge the fierce love of a steadfast Highlander and remorseful but determined Englishman. Will destiny find a way to bring two star-crossed souls together?

A Wallflower's Wassail Punch #8

Lady Annette's first Season was a disaster after a duke's son pinched her by the punchbowl, and she walloped him in the nose. Five years of malicious rumors later, her father offers an outrageous dowry so he too can marry.

Lord Wilkinson, a widower, meets a striking, intelligent woman, with a dry wit only he seems to appreciate. His heart stirs for the first time in decades. But will their age difference and wagging tongues interfere with their budding romance?

The Scoundrel's Christmas Challenge #9

A contest to win her fortune...

Lady Winfield, a long-time wealthy widow, is infamous for her outrageous house parties. While hosting her annual Christmastide gathering, Christiana proposes a new game: a daily challenge of her choice. She will accept the proposal of the man who can best her at three or more competitions by Twelfth Night. Though all agree to the diversion, no one expects the games to include marksmanship, archery, and fencing.

A contest to win her heart...

When Lucius, Viscount Bolingbroke presents Lady Winfield with a secret challenge, she can't resist. Will their midnight rendezvous and private contests end in certain victory for one or a dual attraction for both?

The Duplicate Duke #10

In a country far, far away...

Lady Gwendolyn Beaumaris and her brother have been known as the Downing twins since their father's death when they were eight years old. At twenty-two, Gwen and her mother have settled in Boston while her brother tries to make his fortune in the fur trade. Down to their last pennies, she must consider marriage to a wealthy middle-aged merchant.

The brass ring is so close...

Lord Wickton has worked tirelessly the past two years to bring honor back to the family name. When the viscount learns he is the heir presumptive to his great uncle's dukedom, his prayers are answered.

A comedy of errors...

When a letter arrives announcing that Gwen's brother is the new Duke of Shackerley, mother and daughter come up with a desperate plan: Gwendolyn will impersonate her brother and assume the dukedom. But when the sinfully handsome Wickton meets them at the dock, and Gwen is hopelessly smitten.

A tale of love, deception, and the power of fate will entangle a desperate viscount with a daring female. Can he forgive her charade, or will he snuff out the burning passion that rages in her heart.

Kiss the Scoundrel Farewell #11

Lady Margaret marries out of duty only to find herself in the center of a scandal. Her husband, Baron Drake, dies in a duel over another woman. With no children and no desire to be shackled again, Meg decides to enjoy life as men do. She will be the other woman instead of the wife held captive by the whims of a man. Lady Drake enjoys the freedom of her widow's status.

Simon, Lord Hayward, a dutiful son with no fantasies of love, agrees to marry a wealthy heiress to plump the family's coffers. His father, in love with his mistress for decades, sets out to find his son one of his own. Simon scoffs at the idea, but when he meets an alluring courtesan at a masquerade, he finds himself smitten.

In a twist of fate, the masks come off, and Simon and Meg realize they met years ago, sharing a kiss in a duke's garden. Their secrets come out: She is no courtesan, and he is betrothed. After the viscount confesses his love, the baroness flees for the safety of the countryside.

As Lady Drake begins to doubt her scheme of being a paramour, Lord Hayward wonders if he can be happy with a wife who is not Meg and searches her out. He seeks her out only to find danger lurking in the idyllic English hills, and they soon learn the past has consequences no matter who you pretend to be.

A Paddy's Peelers Mystery series

Set in the hectic district of Cheapside during the Regency, Paddy's Peelers search the dregs of London with skill and cunning to bring criminals to justice and, perhaps, unexpectedly find love along the way. A sweet but action-packed romance.

Crime, Conspiracies, and Courtship #1

Lady Matilda has always been an introvert, preferring her books to awkward conversations with strangers. As her first Season arrives, her mother insists she put away her bluestocking and concentrate on finding a husband. But Mattie is terrified of finding herself betrothed or even worse— not betrothed. The arrogant men of the ton terrify her.

Mr. Harry Walters is an orphaned, ex-Bow Street runner turned investigator, who makes a living by his wits. Working for Paddy O'Brien and his Peelers, often taking assignments for the Home Office, Walters is used to working closely with the beau monde. When a peer approaches him about a new assignment, Harry realizes they are both after the same man. He accepts the job but soon finds himself also protecting the earl's sister.

While working in costume at a masquerade, Walters makes a fatal mistake when he asks Lady Matilda to dance. It takes only a few stolen glances and one waltz for two unlikely souls to become hopelessly entwined. Mattie is determined to win the heart of this handsome, rugged man. Harry is just as determined to keep her safe.

Will fate find a way to bring a common man and an earl's sister a happy ever after? Or will his lack of title and dangerous life keep her at arm's length?

Pads, Purses, and Plum Pudding #2

Dr. Sampson Brooks is on a case that has nothing to do with medicine. He vows to help bring down the man who ruined his father and sent his mother to an early grave. When the villain's top henchmen are apprehended, Sam attends the hanging. While closing one chapter of his story, he unexpectedly opens another.

Dottie Brown, young and naïve, is duped by a charming swindler. A year after the wedding, she learns he's not what he pretends to be. Watching him on the gallows, she vows never to be taken in by romantic notions again. Yet fate tosses two obstacles in her path that day—a handsome physician and an abandoned child.

A chance encounter reveals one woman's secret, another man's revenge, and a love that will change their lives forever.

Poisons, Potions, and Parasols #3

She's content with her life...

Miss Eugenia Chapelle was born on the wrong side of the blanket. After her mother was disowned and fled to London, she pretended to be the widow of a French aristocrat to draw customers as a modiste. After her mother's death, Genie continues the lie, playing the half-French designer of Madame Chapelle's and running the business with her aunt. She never expects an earl to search out his illegitimate daughter twenty-six years later.

He will rip it apart...

Mr. Clayton Pierce works for one of London's most respected

investigators. He has two cases on his docket—tracking a gang of counterfeiters passing banknotes and finding a long-lost child of an earl. When he meets the beautiful and talented Miss Chapelle, his attraction for her is as strong as his obsession with solving mysteries and catching criminals.

After Genie witnesses a possible murder at Hyde Park, she becomes a key witness in his first case. Then, by a twist of fate, she also becomes linked to his second assignment. With danger lurking around every dark corner, and the past the murkiest shadow of all, Clayton learns that solving a case does not always guarantee satisfaction of a job well done. As passions flare and the stakes are raised, will his success as an investigator be his ruin in love?

A MacNaughton Castle Romance series

Highland Regencies

"Witty and sensual!"

Verified Purchase Review

"Lovely characters and complicated family conflicts. You will easily get caught up in their lives."

Goodreads Review

A Merry MacNaughton Mishap (Prequel)

Rone finalist, InD'tale Magazine, N.N. Light Book Heaven finalist

Two feuding clans, one accidental encounter, a wee bit of holiday enchantment…

When Calum MacNaughton rescues a rival clan member from an icy drowning, he is unexpectedly rewarded with the clansman's most precious possession. Now Calum has until Twelfth Night to convince her to stay.

Deception and Desire #1

Nominated for Rone award, InD'tale Magazine, N.N. Light Book Heaven award winner

Two rebellious souls… An innocent deception… One scorching catastrophe…

Fenella Franklin's talents lie in numbers and a keen business mind, not in the art of flirtation. Lachlan MacNaughton has neither the temperament nor the patience to be the next MacNaughton chief, preferring to knock heads together rather than placate bickering clansmen. Their attraction sparks a passion they cannot deny. But will an innocent deception test their newfound love?

Allusive Love #2

A woman in love... An infuriating Scot… A tantalizing chase.

Kirstine has loved Brodie MacNaughton forever, but he considers Kirsty his best friend. When he turns to her for advice, she surprises him with an unexpected kiss that sends fire through his veins. When pride, Highland politics, and tragedy collide, he realizes how precious and allusive true love can be.

A Bonny Pretender #3

She's pretending to be someone she's not… His entire life is based on a lie…

Brigid MacNaughton becomes the perfect lady to placate her family, then falls in love with a quiet, self-possessed Englishman. Lord Raines is smitten with the beguiling and demure Scot. If he divulges his scandalous parentage, will she still fall willingly into his arms? Bonny pretender vs handsome imposter… Can love overcome a double deception?